Ten

By

Prudence MacLeod

This is a work of fiction. Similarities to real people, places, or events are entirely coincidental.

T.E.N.

First edition. November 29, 2023.

ISBN: 978-1927478318

Written by Prudence MacLeod.

Mariena

A soft wind sighed around the decaying buildings and tall structures long since abandoned. Little grew in this area, so most creatures avoided the places of the past occupation. Long ago the people who built the now empty cities left Mariena to explore beyond, but they never returned. Only those who'd served them, and fought them, defeated them, remained.

They were fewer now, the Marienas, and only shadows of what they once were. Whether habit or tradition is not known, but the Marienas always looked to the sky each night. Were they looking for the Gorthas to return, or were they hoping they wouldn't? No matter, the night sky always smiled down on them, until ...

Brainstorming

It's the same in every society, and so it is on the ships of the Wandering Fleet. The explorers and other great commanders, the leaders and heroes do what they do, but they in turn depend on others. The others, the unsung heroes who grow, gather, and prepare the food then clean up after; the cleaners who keep the quarters and corridors clean, those who store and catalogue the supplies, and so on.

For the greats and mighty to do what they do they depend on others to keep things running smoothly, and yet these people have lives too, lives of hope, struggle, success, and failure, of need and fulfilment. Here are a few of those and how they interplay with the greats of the fleet as their combined peoples struggle for survival.

* * * * *

The small fleet of survivors sped through interstellar space on its way toward the next star system they planned to explore. On the home ship, Reacher, a brawl had broken out in the passenger's recreation area between the crews of Orca and Retriever. A few of the SUVI had been enjoying a time of peace together when it happened. As one they rose and waded in, trying to break up the fight before Security forces arrived.

Rayla Mills, commander of Retriever's strike force, found herself being held back by SUVI 20. "Rayla, Rayla, cut it out, calm down."

"Let me go and get the hell out of my way, Twenty."

"Nope, can't do it. Rayla, that was too close, you might have killed him. Get a grip. Here comes Security, just go with them, and don't make a fuss."

"That bastard pulled a knife ..."

"And you broke his arm. Nineteen has his buddies under control, it's over. Deep breaths. Atta girl, now make nice with Security and I'll find Twelve, let her know what happened."

Rayla nodded and allowed the officer to lead her to the brig. The rest of her strike force was there, as were several of the Orca crew with SUVI 19 watching carefully. "All right, men of Orca crew, stay here and I'll come for you in the morning. Right now, I have to go back and smooth this over with the President of the Passenger's Association." With that Nineteen strode away. Several onlookers watched as the unconscious man was carefully lifted onto a stretcher and wheeled away to the infirmary.

* * * * *

The next morning, as the wounded man slowly regained his senses and realized where he was, two women sat in an office chatting; perhaps brainstorming might be a better word. The first was Antha, an Earalithian woman, small of stature as are all her species, and yet exceptionally clever and tenacious. The second was Ebony Graves, a young woman from a failed human colony who had risen dramatically to a command post within the fleet.

Ebony sighed with delight as she finished her tea and set down the cup. "I'm still a bit puzzled."

"Oh? About what?"

"About Igen. I mean, why didn't we just transport those people over to Reacher and adopt them into the fleet, or at least drop them off at the planet. Why leave them on a dying ship?"

Antha smiled. "Ebony, our leaders are so wise. I had a few thoughts on this and asked the vice-admiral about it. She said we couldn't do that at first, they were in the middle of a war and extremely savage. They'd have torn Reacher apart in their desire to make an end of each other.

"Once we got them working together it was easy to see. Their understanding of their reason to exist was to nurture Igen, their religion if you will. Removing them from that ship would be like ripping a babe from the arms of its mother.

"We helped them stop the war and taught them how to care for Igen, that was the motivation for both sides. Now that they have a greater understanding of their situation, they can regain much of their lost knowledge, and yet have a few generations to prepare themselves to abandon that ship, to progress to the next step of their evolution.

"Yes, we've adopted others into the fleet, but each of those groups were already space farers, aware of what we are and what we're trying to do. Those folks on Igen weren't ready for that step, we dared not separate them from their god, the giver and sustainer of life."

"Wow. When you look at it like that, it does make sense," sighed Ebony. "That also makes Captain Sessas even more remarkable in how she's managed to adapt."

"Indeed it does."

Ebony drained the last of her tea then grinned. "So, are you ready to tell me what's on your mind yet?"

Antha smiled. "Can't fool you, can I? Okay, Ebony, I'll talk. I recently discovered something intriguing in the ship's archives. It's something the humans once experimented with in an attempt to help people of diverse backgrounds interact with, and become more comfortable with, each other."

"Okay, so you like this idea, whatever it was, and you think it has possible applications for the fleet. You want to run it past me before taking it to the admiral."

"You know me too well," chuckled Antha. "We're interstellar now, and as ship's counselor, I'm always a lot busier when we're between adventures. Interstellar is boring for you action addicts."

Ebony laughed at that. "Yeah, it can be, all right. So, tell me more, what's the idea?"

"A living library."

"Explain please."

"A living library, a place where I can send a client to help them get more comfortable with other species. It would be manned with volunteers from every species we have in the fleet, human, Earalith, SUVI, Morar, Maccay, and with luck I'll be able to talk Captain Sessas into it as well."

"Okay, so what do these volunteers do there?"

"They talk to the people who come in to talk to them. Like this, you're a human but you struggle a bit with having the Morar around, something about them puts you off. Your therapist, me, has sent you there to meet one and talk to them. The volunteer sits down and talks with you."

"About?"

"Anything at all. The idea is to help you see the volunteer as a person, another living being much like yourself, different in appearance, yes, but underneath the surface differences, the same, just another person trying to survive as best they can, to find joy and meaning in life as are we all. What do you think?"

"Wow, Antha, I think this has a world of potential, but you'll have to be careful who you choose for volunteers, and who you send to them."

"I know. Please understand, I won't send anyone there unless they ask to go. I'll tell them about it but let them make that decision for themselves. Once I'm sure they're ready and want to go, I'll arrange it."

"Sounds good, but I'd add a bit to it, make it more fun."

"Oh? How can we make it more fun?"

"Get lots of volunteers. Picture this, I walk into your living library. A woman greets me there. I say I'm there to talk to a SUVI. She shows me three options, one is a SUVI hunter, another an intuitive, and yet the other something else again. I choose one and they put us together with tea and snacks. I bet I could talk Alli into catering for it."

Antha smiled and sat back in her chair; Ebony shook a finger at her. "Oh, don't look so smug. You knew darn well you'd be able to hook me into running with this thing."

"It's a natural for you, Ebony. Helping people find their place is your passion, and this has Ebony Graves stamped all over it. What do you say, you want to give it a go?"

"You know I do. Okay, first I need to talk to the president of the passenger's association, get her on side and score some space, then I need to call in a few favors to get it set up. Actually, I think I need to run this past the Admiral and Captain Moore, get their take on it.

"Your job will be to point me toward a few likely volunteers. I'll find others and send them to you. You can interview them before we put them to work or not, make sure they're a good fit." She rose to her feet with a smile of anticipation. "Okay, I'm off to track down the admiral."

* * * * *

Meanwhile, the admiral was in a meeting with the captains of the fleet. Suvi-jean Sorenson, Admiral of the Wandering Fleet, was pacing about as usual, trying to calm and organize her thoughts. The captains sat waiting; they'd seen her like this before. Finally, the vice-admiral, Amanda Drake, Suvi-jean's bonded companion and second in command of the fleet, took pity on the others and spoke.

"Admiral?"

"Huh? Oh, sorry people. Yes, I called you here to deal with a growing problem. Things can get a bit out of hand when we're interstellar. Bored people can make mistakes, get up to mischief, and worse. Recently I've noticed a growing issue of racism among the crews. Captain Moore, report."

Rhonda Moore, captain of the Reacher, sighed and nodded. "Aye, Admiral. It happened again last night, another brawl in the passenger area. This time it got a bit ugly. A couple of men from Orca crew started blowing off about the uselessness of having Retriever still active, saying they'd be better able to do the job.

"It went to hell when they made a few nasty remarks about the Retriever's captain. Rayla Mills decked one and the war was on. SUVIs Nine, Sixteen, Nineteen, and Twenty waded in to break it up before Security got there."

"Dammit," snarled Sheila Singh, captain of the Orca, "I'll deal with those fools. Did you get their names?"

"One's in the brig," replied Rhonda, "the other is in medical under guard, Nineteen picked up the rest."

"Medical?"

"Apparently, he pulled a knife on Rayla Mills. She broke him up pretty bad, would have killed him if Twenty hadn't pulled her off."

"Is she in the brig too?" asked the Admiral.

"No longer. She spent the night there cooling off for throwing the first punch, but I won't punish a woman for defending herself. We cut her loose this morning."

"You did right, Rhonda," said Jeannie, and Sheila nodded her agreement. "All right, people, we need to do something about this. It's been happening more and more when we're between systems. I'm wide open to suggestions here."

"Can't force folk to like folk," said Sessas, captain of the Retriever and the only Saurian in the entire fleet. "Try, make worse." That brought a round of agreement from the rest.

"Any suggestions Sessas?" asked Jeannie.

"Ask Antha, Ebony, maybe have idea."

"Good thinking, Captain Sessas," nodded Jeannie, reaching for her comm. "Commander Ebony Graves to the bridge briefing room. Repeat, Commander Ebony Graves to the bridge briefing room."

"On my way, Admiral," came the response from Jeannie's shoulder pin.

"While we wait for her to arrive, I have another suggestion. Sheila, I understand yours is the main war ship, and I know you've molded that crew into an efficient unit, a ship of warriors. Now you need to go to the next step."

"Make those hardheaded fools understand the rest of the population is who we're defending, keeping safe. They will never feel safe, fully trust us, if this crap keeps happening. I understand, Jeannie, and I've been working on it. I'll admit I could use help with this. I'm wide open to suggestions."

"I have one," said Hal White, Security Chief for the Reacher and commander of the fighter ship, EX4.

"Let's hear it, Hal," said Sheila.

"Give the job to Nineteen. When the admiral first arrived on the Reacher I was wearing the same attitude those guys are. I was armed and in full armor, yet she beat the snot out of me, removing the ego issue. In the days and weeks that followed I saw how she used her superior abilities to nurture and protect the rest of us, not go on an ego trip showing off her superiority."

Sheila nodded. "Nineteen huh? Why not. I'll see what he has to say about it."

At that point Ebony arrived. "You called for me, Admiral?"

"Indeed we did, Ebony. Please, sit down. Now here's the problem we want your input with."

As she sat listening, Ebony's grin grew wider. "I see. Admiral, I was actually looking for you to run an idea past you. Antha got me interested in this earlier today, but I wanted your input and permission before running with it." She continued to outline the idea of a living library for them.

When she finished Jeannie nodded. "I get it, Ebony. It's a lot harder to feel superior to someone who you know personally and like. If we can get some of the more troublesome types involved with this it could be a big help. What do you think, Captains?"

"I like it," said Captain Baris, Jeannie's grandfather, and captain of the salvage ship Recovery Two.

"I once visited such a place on old Earth," smiled Olga Volkov, captain of Recovery One. "It was indeed an eye-opening experience."

Rhonda Moore smiled as she spoke. "I like it. I say set it up then we send some of our tough characters for a visit."

"Can't," said Captain Sessas.

"Why not, Sessas?" asked Sheila.

"Is punishment. Make angrier, blame victim, blame you, resent everybody. Must decide to go themselves. They go, they learn, share with others on crew. Much better."

"She's right," said Ebony. "You can tell them about it, suggest they might give it a try, but no more. They'll have to go to Antha and ask to go."

"Each step is a step forward," sighed Jeannie. "Do it, Ebony. Let us know when you're ready for visitors."

"Thank you, Admiral. With your permission I'll be about the task." At Jeannie's nod Ebony rose and left the room.

* * * * *

While Ebony sought out her companion, Ensign Brie Elliot, and explained the new project, the Marienas came out to gaze at the sky. Suddenly, as one, they turned their gaze toward a new direction, a new part of the sky near the horizon. Something, or someone, was coming.

"Are they returning, do you think?" The question ran through the assembly of creatures as they faced the new direction.

"Perhaps, but more likely something new. We should let them explore while we observe, explore the possibilities, test them, find the weaknesses, and then destroy them, send them away never to return."

A general humming sound of agreement was heard. "Hmmmmm."

"We will not serve them."

"No, that we will not do, but we will test them, find the weaknesses, drive them out never to return." Again the hum of general consensus sounded over the landscape. They searched the memories left to them by the ancestors, seeking and reviewing the methods of testing, clouding the mind of another creature while inflicting damage to the being's systems, searching out weaknesses, judging their worth, preparing for the battle of survival, of dominance.

Getting Ready

The mess was a busy place as SUVI 10 and her three companions entered. They gathered their trays and headed for what looked like an open spot at a table. SUVI 10 had a unique affinity for plant life and had been the main gardener on Elysium. She now spent her time in Hydroponics and on other projects concerning the plants and soils brought back to the ship by the explorers.

Chatting among themselves they approached and sat, or at least Ten tried. She glanced up as SUVI 12 called out a greeting then a small hand slapped her hard.

"Hey, watch what the hell you're doing. You almost sat on me."

Startled, Ten jumped back and turned, her fist stopping mere inches from the small Earalithian woman face. "Oh gods, I'm so sorry," babbled Ten as she jerked her hand back and shoved her tray aside, away from the angry woman.

"So you should be, you great oaf, you could have squashed me flat."

In spite of herself, Ten started to grin. "Oh come on, you're not that small. I truly am sorry I almost hurt you."

"Well you did. I'm not that small? You're one of those super SUVI, knows everything, can do everything better than anybody else, yet you didn't know I was here? Really?"

Ten sighed and sat down, her meal forgotten. "Yes, I'm SUVI, but no, I'm not one of the super SUVI. I'm not intuitive, I'm not a hunter, and I honestly didn't see you there. Again, I'm so sorry I nearly hurt you."

"Forget it; just forget it. I'm outta here." The small woman stood up, gathered her tray, and marched off. Ten sat watching her go, a strange sad look on her face.

"Ten, you all right?" asked Lilly Peters, second in command on the explorer ship EX2. Lilly was a botanist and they'd been discussing crop rotation in hydroponics as they walked in.

"Huh? Oh, sure, I'm good, just a bit distracted, I guess."

"Ten, what is it?"

SUVI 10 sighed and leaned her elbows on the table. "Sorry. I haven't been spoken to like that since we left the Caverns on Elysium, and I reacted badly, nearly hit her. It just shook me a bit. I guess I really scared her, that's probably why she was so angry."

"Are you sure you're okay?"

"Yeah, I'm fine, Lilly."

"If you say so."

"Hi there, friendly people, what's new and exciting?" asked SUVI 12 as she sat with them.

"Ten's made a new friend," said one of the others at the long table.

"Oh? What happened?"

"We were talking about those bushes we picked up on Igen," replied Lilly. "Ten was listening to me and didn't see an Earalithian woman arrive at the table. She nearly sat on her, and the woman slapped her pretty hard."

"That could have gone ugly," said Twelve. "What happened? Are you okay, Ten?"

"Yeah, I'm good. Aw, I nearly hit her, Twelve," sighed Ten. "You know what it's like, you get startled and you react, that's how you stay alive on Elysium. All the humans knew enough to never touch one of us by surprise. Anyway, I didn't hurt her, and I tried to apologize ..."

"But?"

"It was like I was suddenly back in the Caverns, facing an angry woman. She chewed me out good then walked away."

"Ah-huh. So then what?"

"Then nothing," replied Ten, gazing at her hands.

Twelve looked at her for a long moment then reached for those hands. "Aw hell no. Ten, tell me no."

"Can't, wish I could, but I can't. Now what the hell am I going to do?"

Suvi 12 sighed and gave those hands a gentle squeeze then sat back. "I'd say your best bet would be Antha for a start."

Ten nodded and sighed. "You're probably right about that. Guess I'll go see if she's in her office." With that she rose and walked dejectedly away, leaving her tray abandoned on the table.

Lilly turned to Twelve with a raised eyebrow. "Twelve, what the hell just happened?"

"It's a SUVI thing."

"And none of my business. Understood."

"No, Commander, it's not like that. You're from the Caverns too, so you know why Ten reacted the way she did."

"I get that part, but there's more going on here, isn't there?"

"There is, but that's the part that's not our business. I understand what happened here for Ten, but I can't help her, neither can you, and we need to stay out of it unless Ten asks for our input."

"So, it's a SUVI thing I wouldn't understand."

"You might intellectually, but not truly. Hell, we don't really understand it either."

"It must be so hard for you guys," said Lilly. "You were all so tightly controlled, and now you're free to explore who and what you are, but none of you have any idea what you really are, and you have no elders to teach you."

"Yeah, that pretty much sums it up."

"Twelve, keep a sisterly eye out for her?"

"I will. Actually, I'm starting to think I should have sent her to Twenty. Ah well, she'll figure that part out on her own I guess."

* * * * *

SUVI 10 sat in Antha's office, staring at her hands. Antha, ship's counsellor on the Reacher, sipped at her tea, waiting patiently for the woman to be ready to speak. Finally, her patience was rewarded. "Antha, tell me you Earalithian women are a forgiving people."

Antha set down her teacup and leaned her arms on the desk. "Some are, some aren't. What happened, Ten?"

Ten sighed and looked away as she spoke. "It was in the mess. Commander Peters and I were talking about the possibility of rotating some of the crops in Hydroponics. She was speaking and I was listening to her, not paying attention to what I was doing as we got to the table. I almost sat on a woman, one of the Earalithians.

"She was really angry, perhaps scared would be a better word. She chewed me out big time and wouldn't hear an apology. I did try, but she stormed away. I don't think she likes the SUVI and that didn't help any."

"I see. Ten, I wouldn't make too much of it. I'm sure she'll get over it when she calms down. Give it a day or two then approach her with that apology."

"You think that'll work?"

"It should. Ten, this seems to be quite important to you. May I ask why?"

Again Ten looked away before speaking. "It's a SUVI thing." Antha remained silent so reluctantly, she continued. "You can't ever tell anyone about this."

Antha switched off the recording device. "Strictest confidence, I swear it."

Ten sighed and went on. "We SUVI didn't know about this, none of us. Our experiences on Elysium prevented it from ever manifesting. As you know, everything about the SUVI seems to be magnified."

Antha nodded her understanding so Ten went on. "Everything is magnified, including the desire to mate. It never manifested on Elysium because of the abuse we endured, the way we were forced to live. I guess enough stress will shut it off. Anyway, a SUVI will instinctively choose a mate, and from that point on the need for the chosen one will be their driving force unless some danger presents itself.

"The first to encounter this was SUVI 5 when she first appeared on the Reacher, but she didn't know what it was. Eighteen fell next when she was assigned to work with Captain da Silva. Twenty was hit with it when she and Commander White were lost on Planet Stormy. Thirteen fell as soon as Connie was assigned to EX2. By then we were starting to figure it out. Twelve's experience on Igen when she found and rescued Rayla cinched it.

"We SUVI have a built-in mating instinct that, once triggered can't be reversed."

"Oh dear, and you instinctively responded to this Earalithian woman?"

"Yeah, I did. She hit me, triggering a defensive reflex, but I got myself stopped before I hurt her. She was so angry, frightened, and so utterly adorable I started to smile."

"Oops."

Ten finally chuckled. "Yeah, oops. That was the wrong thing to do, it just made her angrier. So, here's me, hopelessly pining for a fierce little woman who is scared to death of me and mad at me to boot. Worse, I don't even know her name.

"So, any advice for a love struck SUVI?"

"As much as I'd love to rush out and find her for you, Ten, I can't get involved here. Having said that, there are options and possibilities. First, keep an eye out for her, give it a day or two then if you see her, try a gentle approach, and see how it goes. Second, Talk to Ebony Graves, she's got something interesting in the works that might help."

"Oh?"

"Yes. It's a living library, a place where you can go to talk to other people, people you know nothing about, people that perhaps make you uneasy or nervous. She'll be needing volunteers and I'm sure a SUVI would be a big help."

"In what way?"

Antha smiled. "You're a new species, completely unknown, the ultimate enigma. I'm sure if you volunteer, you'll get lots of people curious about your people."

"What would I say to them, tell them about us?"

"No, no, you won't have to try to explain the SUVI, that's not the idea. The idea is for people to talk to you, so they understand you're just like them, a person trying to survive and thrive, find her way through the maze called life. They learn to see you as a person, and you learn the same about them."

"Wow, that could be interesting at that. All right, I'll see if I can track down Commander Graves. Give it a couple of days then try the apology again, huh? Okay, I'll do it. Thanks, Antha."

"All my pleasure, Ten. Good luck."

* * * * *

While Ten went looking for Antha, Soran sat in her quarters trying to get a grip on her emotions. A soft tap came at the door. "Go away."

"Soran, It's Tagora."

"Okay, come in."

Soran's best friend, and fellow crew member on the Friendship, stepped quietly into the room and closed the door behind her. "Honey, are you all right? I saw you running back here, crying."

"Yeah, I'm okay, just a bit shook up."

Tagora sat beside her and put a friendly arm around her shoulders. "What happened?"

"I nearly got killed, that's what happened. I was in the mess, trying to get something to eat. I sat down and the next thing you know one of those giant SUVI nearly sat on me. I'd have been squished if I hadn't smacked her.

"By all the spirits I've never seen anything move that fast. Her supersized fist was right at my face before I could blink."

"Oh gods, did she hit you?"

"No, no, she didn't. No, she went all contrite and tried to apologize, but I was so scared I just yelled at her and stormed away then ran back here to cry my eyes out. They're so damn big and strong and scary ..."

"Easy now, honey, easy. The SUVI would never hurt you. Think about Eighteen, she's always on the ship with us and she like our big sister."

"Yeah, I guess, but she's a more normal size and she doesn't ... I panicked huh?"

Tagora chuckled at that. "I wouldn't say panicked, overreacted a bit maybe. You were scared, honey, that's understandable."

"So, what should I do now? There were other SUVI there; they probably think I hate them all now."

"Do you?"

"What? No, why would you even ask me that."

"You shy away from them all the time. I know Eighteen has noticed it."

"I don't hate them, Taggie, honestly I don't. It's just that they're so damn fast and strong, they scare me."

"Honey, what aren't you telling me? Why do the SUVI scare you so badly?"

"They all do, SUVI, humans, Morar, we're the smallest and weakest. Any one of them could ..." She began to tremble and Tagora tightened the arm around her shoulders. "When I was little my oldest brother used to hurt me just to make me cry. When I escaped to the colony, I thought I was finally free of all that, and then I married Rotan. He beat me. Does it make me evil that I'm glad he couldn't be revived?"

"No, honey, it doesn't, it just makes you a woman who's been hurt too much too often."

"So, what should I do?"

"About?"

"The SUVI I yelled at, all of them maybe?"

"Honey, I think this goes a bit deeper than that for you. I think you should talk to Antha, let her help you work through some of this older stuff. About the SUVI? If you see her again, maybe approach and apologize for yelling at her."

"But I didn't do anything wrong, she's the one who nearly killed me."

"It's not always about being right, or justified, honey. Sometimes it's about making peace with another tormented soul."

"What?"

"You've had bad experiences with others who were more powerful than you. The SUVI were slaves; I'm sure whoever that was, she would be able to understand how it feels to be the weaker one, the one unfairly abused."

"Yeah, maybe you're right. Okay, I'll see if Antha has time for me. Thanks for helping me calm down."

"All my pleasure. You okay now?"

"Yeah, my heart rate is back to normal, and the shakes have stopped, I'll be fine."

"All right then, I'd better scoot to the ship, I'm on watch tonight."

"Yeah, keep an eye out for all those alien attackers trying to get into the Reacher's cargo bay."

Tagora giggled as she left Soran in her quarters. Early the next morning Soran was in Antha's office and SUVI 10 was in Ebony's.

Hard Lesson

It was early, but the five men in full armor stood at attention, waiting the captain's pleasure. She took her time, her back to them. Slowly Sheila Singh, captain of the war ship Orca, turned to face them. "You five men were involved in a recent incident aboard the Reacher. As I understand it, you declared yourselves superior to the strikers of Retriever. They proved you wrong." Shame faced none would meet her penetrating gaze. "Stay at attention, eyes front." They brought themselves back to attention.

"Better." She sighed deeply. "Gentlemen, I've gone over the visual records of that encounter, as well as what audio could be gathered. I'm deeply disappointed. I personally chose ever member of this crew because I thought they were the best, the most likely to succeed, the most likely to keep us all alive in a combat situation.

"Your actions aboard the Reacher point out clearly where I failed. Yes, you are members of the most disciplined fighting force humanity has ever produced, but you have failed to understand the true purpose of this force, the purpose of this ship. Our purpose is to protect the fleet, to defeat any enemies that appear, yes.

"However, that does not make us superior beings. Just because we're part of the most numerous species, humans, doesn't make us superior to any of the others, and I will not tolerate anyone disparaging any of the other races. To bring home this point to you five, I now present your new instructor, a truly superior being, and a member of a different species. SUVI 19, will you please explain to these men the true purpose of this crew, this ship?"

"I'd be happy to, and thank you, Captain." As he stepped forward the captain turned on her heel and left the exercise area, leaving the men to face their fate. She grinned to herself as she left the room. Those men were about to get an attitude adjustment.

Back in the exercise area Nineteen was pacing. Finally he stopped and cast aside his tunic, facing the men with bare hands. "Come at me."

Wide eyed they all stared at him. "Sir?"

"Don't call me sir, I hold no rank here. My name is SUVI 19, and by your own clearly stated standards, inferior to you. There are five of you in full armor, come at me, demonstrate your superiority. Do it or I'll come at you, and you won't like it."

Swallowing hard, they spread out to surround him. Nineteen laughed as they moved slowly. "On Elysium you'd all be dead if you faced a garog like that." With that he moved. Within seconds they were all down and he stood over them shaking his head.

To their amazement he helped them back to their feet. "Now that we have that out of the way, I'll tell you why you're really here," he said as he pulled his tunic back on. "The captain asked me to take the attitude out of you, to show you what a superior being is capable of, but I don't think that was necessary. In fact, I think it was a waste of time, except that it allowed me to get some real exercise without actually hurting anybody."

"Says you," grumbled one of the men.

Nineteen chuckled at that. "Look men, I know how it is, and I agree with you in that I believe the crew of the Orca is second to none. The problem here is old habits, old human training habits. I was classically trained at security even as you were trained in classic military style. It makes you a superior fighter, a member of an elite group, and you're entitled to feel pride in that.

"What got lost here, as the captain has pointed out, is the true purpose of this ship and crew. I've been given the task of correcting this and I want you five to help me, to be my own special elite group, true leaders of this crew. So, are you game for that?"

They looked at each other then back to him. "Yeah, I guess so, as long as you're not going to beat the crap out of us again."

"Deal," he grinned. "Prepare to live life the way of the SUVI."

"The way of the SUVI?"

"Yes, the way of the SUVI. We SUVI all know we're superior physical beings, but there's more. We're herd animals, and as such, the needs of the herd come before our own desires unless there's a clear threat to the individual's survival. We're superior, yes, but that doesn't give us permission to be bullies, be arrogant, to throw our weight around, it gives us a purpose, to serve and protect the others."

They paused to think about what he had said then one spoke. "So, you're saying we failed as superior crew by having a few drinks and running off at the mouth."

"Yes, that's what I'm saying. When was the last time a SUVI pushed you around?"

"About two minutes ago," grinned one man. "So, we have to let go of some of that training."

"Not so much the training," said Nineteen, "just the attitude. Oh, and be thankful it was me you faced today. The captain would have seriously kicked your ass."

There were a few rueful chuckles at that. "Okay, Nineteen, we're in. What do you want us to do?"

"That's great, I'm proud of you already. Here's the first step, and it's a hard one, but I'll be doing it too. Commander Graves is building a living library. It works like this, you go there and pick a person from another ship, or race, one you don't like, and talk to them, listen to them, try to understand what makes them tick.

"Once you've got a handle on it, try to see how you can make their life easier for them, that's service, that's what we do best, that's what we do over and above our job on the ship, that's why we trained ourselves to this level in the first place. Moreover, that's what will make the captain proud of us instead of looking for our scalps. We do what we do for the greater good. That's our mantra, for the greater good. So, you still game?"

"Yeah, we're in. How do we go about signing up for this living library?"

"You book an appointment with Antha, she'll set you up, or send you away if she doesn't think it's right for you or if you're not really ..."

"Okay Nineteen, we get it," said one. "I'll go. I guess I'll ask for a Morar, see what they're all about."

"Yeah, I'm in," agreed another. "Maybe I'll ask for the Captain of the Retriever if that's possible. I'd like to know what makes that one tick."

"That's an easy one," chuckled Nineteen, "she works like a SUVI. Protect the clan, that's why she was on that ship in the first place. All right, you guys get the idea. I'll leave you to it then we'll meet in the mess six days from now and debrief, see how we're doing."

"Can I ask you something, Nineteen?" asked one man as they turned to go.

"Sure."

"Who are you going to ask to talk to?"

"One of the Maccay," sighed Nineteen. "Intrusive little buggers, always poking into everything. They make me nervous." The men chuckled as he walked away. "Remember, for the greater good."

* * * * *

Commander Rayla Mills stood at attention on the bridge of the Retriever while the captain paced. They were alone on the ship as it was in the cargo bay of the Reacher. Finally, Captain Sessas stopped pacing and faced Rayla. "I saw video. You threw first punch."

"Yes Captain."

"Why?" She got no response, nor would Rayla make eye contact. Sessas tried again. "Why hit man? What happen to make you fight man?"

Rayla sighed. "They were making nasty comments about the Retriever."

"So you hit them?"

"Not then."

"When?"

"When they made nasty comments about my captain."

She was surprised to hear the captain's hissing laughter. "You think they learn anything?"

"They learned not to do it where I can hear them," sighed Rayla.

"Rayla learn anything?"

"I still need to work on my temper?"

Again came that hissing laughter. "Is good to learn from mistake." She paced around for a moment then faced Rayla again. "You good leader for Strikers, you defend ship, captain. Now need to work on temper. You go. Tell everybody captain chew out good."

"That's it?"

"Rayla, you spend night in brig for punch, is okay. You break arm for knife, is good. I watch, I see. Man not know you pull back killing blow, but Sessas see on video. You go. No mark on record."

Barely believing what she'd just heard, Rayla thanked her then retreated from the ship to her quarters and the arms of her lover. "Wow," she sighed. "There's more to the captain than any of us realize. She saw me turn his knife to his heart then pull back."

"Why did you pull back, Ray?" asked SUVI 12. "That move should have been an instinct with you."

"It was, but I was able to override the instinct even in a fight. All that SUVI training you've been doing with me must be working."

"Yes, to survive as a hunter you have to think faster than the instinct, change the action on the fly as needed. Well done. I'm quite proud of you, my precious girl." Rayla sighed and snuggled deeper into Twelve's embrace.

* * * * *

While the men of the Orca were getting some instruction SUVI style, and Rayla faced her captain for discipline, Soran sat in Antha's office, staring at her hands. Antha sat waiting.

Finally, Soran cracked. "It wasn't my fault."

"Tell me what happened."

"I was in the mess and a SUVI nearly sat on me."

"And?" prompted Antha.

"And I slapped her and yelled at her. I startled her and she nearly hit me."

"Oh?"

"Yeah. By all the spirits, Antha, I wouldn't have believed anything could move that fast. Before I could blink my eyes I was staring at a fist the size of a door right at the end of my nose."

"But she didn't hit you?"

"No, she didn't. I guess I startled her, and she reacted instinctively. She got stopped then tried to apologize, but I was so angry I wouldn't listen. I just yelled at her some more then stomped away."

Antha set her tea mug down and smiled gently. "Angry or frightened?"

Soran looked away and sighed. "Scared to death, Antha. When I was young my brother used to torture me to make me scream. After I escaped to the colony I bonded with Rotan, but he started beating me. Nobody cared, nobody would help me. I tried to run away, but he caught me every time. I'm glad they couldn't revive him."

"You've been hurt, a lot, and this SUVI woman frightened you. Can you tell me what she did after she nearly hit you?"

"She tried to apologize, but I could see the smirk on her face. She thought it was funny."

"Are you sure about that? Did her apology not seem sincere?"

"Well, okay, it did, but she was smiling. She tried not to, but I could tell." Antha didn't reply, just sat waiting. "Okay, I don't know, I thought she was laughing at me. You know, the tiny creature that roars at the big predator to scare them away."

"Is that how you see the SUVI? As predators?"

"Yeah, well, no; I don't know. I guess not. I need to toughen up huh?"

"No, girl, you do need to face some of your fear, but in a safe way."

"Okay, so how do I do that?"

"You say this happened in the mess. Perhaps if you see her there again you could approach her, talk to her."

"What would I say to her?"

"Apologize for yelling at her?"

"Me? Why should I apologize? She's the one who nearly sat on me."

"Do you think she did it on purpose?"

"No."

"So?"

"Okay, if I see her I'll try, but if she kills me I swear I'll haunt you for the rest of your days."

"Duly noted," grinned Antha. "Soran, I've found all the SUVI to be approachable. Do it in the mess or someplace with a lot of people around so you feel safe."

Soran sighed and nodded as she rose and left the office. "Okay." She headed back toward her quarters, mulling over what Antha had said.

* * * * *

As Soran left Antha's office and Rayla returned to the arms of her lover, the fleet dropped to sub-light speed in a new system. On the only planet in the Goldilocks Zone the Marienas gazed as one at a single point in the sky, a new pinpoint of light had appeared, and then another and another. A shiver of fear and resolve as well as excited anticipation ran through them. It would soon be time to test their own mettle as well as that of the intruders.

Arrival

"Fleet has arrived Admiral," said Captain Rhonda Moore of the Retriever.

Admiral Suvi-jean Sorenson nodded. "Fleet all stop."

"All stop aye," replied Rhonda as she nodded to the second officer and the command went out to all ships. "Fleet has stopped, Admiral."

"Launch Probe."

"Probie is away, Admiral."

"Excellent. So, now we wait. I think I'll check in with Ebony; see how that new project is going." She turned and left the bridge, reaching for her comm. "Sorenson to Commander Ebony Graves."

"Here, Admiral," came the cheerful reply.

"Care to meet me in Simple Pleasures for a snack and an update on that new project?"

"On my way."

"Sorenson to Vice-admiral Drake."

"Here, Admiral."

"I'm meeting with Ebony in Simple Pleasures. Would you like to sit in on her update?"

"You know I would; I'll be right there."

The admiral arrived to find Ebony and Amanda waiting outside. They went in to find a table ready with their favorite tea and the manager's latest recipe ready for a test taste. Jeannie smiled and spoke as they sat at the table. "You know, Ebony, since you set this place up for your genius friend I've had to double my exercise program."

"Me too," chuckled Ebony, "but it's worth it. Just taste these tarts."

Amanda moaned with delight at the first bite then nodded her approval. "So, Ebony, what's the good word on the living library? Are you having any luck finding volunteers?"

"Way too much, actually. We've had to turn a number of folks away."

"Oh, why?" asked Jeannie.

"That one's Antha's call. The idea here is to connect people with others they don't understand, or don't like, to give them a different perspective. Some of those who volunteered were a bit thin skinned, so to speak. However, we've got a lot of good folks ready, so the plan is to rotate them in and out as time and availability permit."

"Sounds good," said Amanda. "Got any customers lined up?"

"Yeah, we have, more than I would have thought at first. Antha's been pretty choosy about who she'll send to us, but we're about set to give it a go as soon as we're ready to leave this system."

"Why wait?" asked Jeannie, taking a sip of her tea and moaning with delight.

"I thought that most of the people who needed to be involved would be on assignment, you know, hunting and gathering, that sort of thing."

Jeannie smiled at that and set her teacup back on the table. "I wouldn't wait, Ebony. This needs to happen, the sooner the better. Schedule as many as you can while we're in this system then see how it's working."

"This one's really got you intrigued, hasn't it?" grinned Amanda.

"Okay, yes it has," admitted Jeannie. "This has the potential to defuse a lot of tensions in the fleet, and I want to see it succeed. It's also given me another idea to bring to the captains. Call a meeting of the captains and I'll run it by them while we wait for Probie to report in."

"And so to work," smiled Amanda as she rose and reached for her comm.

Ebony rose as well. "I'll see if I can get a few folks together today, Admiral."

"And I'll go give our compliments to the chef then chastise her for expanding my waistline before I head to the briefing room," grinned Jeannie.

* * * * *

As usual, Admiral Sorenson was pacing while she waited for the captains to gather. "Everybody's here, Admiral."

"Thank you, Vice-Admiral. People, Amanda and I have just spent some time with Ebony, and she has her living library ready to go. This also gave me an idea, another way we might diffuse tensions between the races and crews. I wouldn't want to do this under stressful conditions, but when we reach a dead system it could be interesting.

"Here's the idea, mix up the crews a bit. Say, take the engineer from EX2 and put him on Retriever. Put Retriever's engineer on F1, etc. We couldn't do things like this under combat or alert conditions of course, but during some of the down times it could prove interesting. Don't be shy, captains, give me your thoughts on this."

Only silence greeted her idea. "Come on, come on, don't all jump at once." She sighed and settled back into her chair beside Amanda. "Bad idea, huh?"

"I don't know," chuckled Captain Baris of Recovery 2. "It could have possibilities."

"I send Kumar to Reacher, be first officer," said Sessas. "Rhonda sent Jake to Retriever, keep Tentee out of trouble."

Jeannie smiled at Sessas. "All right, Captain Sessas, I get the message. Take your time, people, mull it over for a few days, give Ebony's library a chance to take hold, then we can take another look at it."

* * * * *

Down on the planet they were approaching, the Marienas waited nervously; the simple peace of their world was about to be shattered, for good or ill they could not know. Silently the few who watched the daytime skies wandered the overgrown streets, following well-worn paths around fallen structures, searching the skies with their eyes, and the memories their ancestors had passed to them.

A soft rain fell on the tall female as she searched the skies, but her gaze could not penetrate the clouds. She sent out a query to others and it was relayed to faraway places, but none saw any movement that should not be. Mourana sighed and allowed her awareness to return to the broken city and the gentle falling rain. With a wistful sigh she allowed the rain to nourish her.

Later, as the day faded and the rest of the Marienas emerged to gaze at the sky, the thought was formed. "What shall we do when they come?" It rippled through the general consciousness until an answer was achieved. "We will greet them, welcome them, test them, but we will not serve them."

"Who will speak for us?" Again, the thought spread through the collective and back until the response was clearly decided. "Mourana will express our thoughts, discover what we need to know, keep them distracted while we test them."

"Who will speak for them?" This one took longer to decide, but at last the thought circulated. "Whichever one we choose."

"The memories of the ancestors show weapons that bring death and pain. How do we avoid this?"

"The weapons cannot harm what they cannot find, what they do not know is there before them. We have no wish to harm them excessively, just to test them, but we will not allow them to harm us as the Gorthas once did to the ancestors. We have evolved ways to avoid this. We will test them, learn what we need to know, and then use that knowledge to drive them away permanently."

"So all is decided? Then now we await the arrival of the unknown."

* * * * *

On the Reacher, SUVI 18 sought out the admiral, SUVI 5. "You're looking for me, Eighteen?"

"I am, yes."

"It's about the planet?"

"Yes. I'm getting some threat, but more waves of fear, resentment, and defiance."

"I see, but no real threat?"

"It's hard to tell, but I don't really think so, not at first anyway."

"What do you recommend?"

"Send Ten down for a look."

"Ten?"

"Five, I have no idea why, but I get the sense Ten should be the first one on that planet. I believe her affinity for plant life will be the most helpful here."

"So, you think we'll encounter intelligent plant life?"

Eighteen chuckled at that. "I have no real idea, just giving you my impressions."

"All right, now you have me utterly intrigued. I'll talk to Ten and Captain Morthel, arrange it and we'll see what wonders unfold. Thank you for this, Eighteen." The woman smiled and nodded then returned to the office she shared with her partner, Captain Linsey da Silva.

SUVI 10 smiled bemusedly at the admiral. "Seriously? Intelligent plant life?"

"She couldn't say," chuckled Suvi-jean, "just that she had a strong feeling you should be the first to set foot on the planet. What do you say, are you up for it?"

"Absolutely. I've been trying to talk Lilly into taking me along on some of these trips. I'm in."

"Then head to the mess and grab a bite. Probie should be back any minute now and Morthel is already fussing, ready to go. I'll let her know you're coming."

A few moments later Ten was in the mess wolfing down a sandwich. A small Earalithian woman swallowed hard then began to approach her. However, the meeting was not to be as the call came over the speakers. "EX2 crew to the ship, repeat, EX2 crew to the ship." SUVI 10 jumped up and fled the mess leaving a disappointed, and yet relieved, Soren standing alone near the recently abandoned table.

* * * * *

"All crew aboard, Captain Morthel."

"Thank you, Commander Peters. Close her up. Launch when ready, Three."

"Launching. Ship is in space, Captain."

"Head for the planet in the Goldilocks zone, Three. Attention crew, for this little adventure we have an additional crew member. SUVI 10 will be the first to set foot on this planet."

Thirteen raised an eyebrow at Ten. "Eighteen had a hunch," chuckled Ten.

"Good enough for me," grinned Thirteen.

"Well, since you're the new first explorer, Ten," smiled Lilly, "you can watch the sensors, see what's down there then pick a spot to check out."

"Sensors it is," replied Ten. "Exactly what am I looking for?"

"Anything and everything interesting," said the captain. "We'll do a full grid search before we do any walkabout."

The small ship swept down on the lonely planet then leveled out about a kilometer above the surface. "Grid pattern established, Captain. Proceeding as per established protocols."

Empty but Not

For two days the explorer ship flew slowly over Mariena, carefully logging the terrain. "Getting bored Ten?" smiled the captain.

Ten chuckled at that. "Yes, a bit, but more anxious to get down there and have a look firsthand."

"Well, the atmosphere is breathable with the filters, so pick a likely spot and we'll go down for a look."

"Can we go back to the place we saw those ruins? There was something about that place."

"Oh?" asked the captain as she pointed at the pilot who grinned and turned the ship north toward the ruins.

"Yes. A city of that size would have farmlands nearby. That would be a natural and a good place to start checking for edible plants."

"Understood," replied Captain Morthel. "However, considering why you're with us this time, I recommend caution before Lilly starts gathering samples."

"Ship has arrived, Captain."

"Thank you, Three. All right, Ten, pick your spot."

"There I think," she mused as she swept the cross hairs over the screen to rest on an open area near a fallen building. She pressed the switch to send those coordinates to the pilot station. A moment later the ship sank gracefully to the ground.

"Ship has landed, Captain."

"Thank you, Three. Connie?"

"Looks good from here, Captain," replied the Security Officer. "Thirteen?"

"Not my job this time," he grinned. "Ask Ten. Time to check the gardens, Ten."

"What does that mean?" asked Morthel.

"On Elysium I was usually the one sent to tend the garden on the planet's surface," replied SUVI 10. "I have a strong affinity for edible plants. The virus that made us was endemic to an herbivorous species. I have no idea where these super hunters came from."

Thirteen chuckled at her and gestured to the hatch. "Mind if this old hunter tags along, you know, just in case I might learn something new."

"Or in case something tried to eat me for breakfast. Whenever you're ready, Captain."

"Drop shields."

"Shields down, Captain."

"All yours, Ten."

"Thank you, Captain. Come on, Thirteen, let's go exploring." Ten fitted the air filters into her nose, the hatch swung open, and they stepped out together. Watching the two SUVI, the captain nodded her approval. SUVI 10 was grinning with delight as she stepped slowly and carefully toward a clump of scarlet foliage. Thirteen stayed a step behind her, senses on full alert, his eyes sweeping the area constantly searching for a threat, any threat.

Ten inspected several different types of plant life, but nothing more happened. Eventually she sat down and placed her hands on the ground and spoke. "I know you're here; I can feel you through the ground. Please come out and talk to me."

As she spoke, something moved in the shadows, seeming to materialize among the trees, there and yet, not there. Ten reeled as her mind was assaulted with visions and waves of defiance. She screamed and grabbed at her head; the visions stopped.

Thirteen was instantly at her side, his weapon aimed at the form in the trees. "Ten?"

"No, it's all right. Let me try again." Reluctantly, he stepped back but didn't lower the weapon.

Ten drew a deep breath then placed her hands on the ground again. "Go slower. Please go slower so I can understand you." She reeled as the visions returned, much slower this time. She saw two species of aliens, one torturing the others, forcing them to work then killing them for food. "I understand."

"How can you hope to understand?" belled a voice in her mind.

"I was once the same," she replied. "I'll try to show you." Ten began to form visual memories of her youth on Elysium. Suddenly her memories, and the emotions were all dragged out of her at once. With a wail of pure torment she leaped to her feet to break the connection to the creature.

Thirteen's weapon fired but Ten knocked the barrel up to spoil his aim. "No, don't. Just hold me for a minute."

She was instantly in his arms. "I've got you, my sister. Feel me, I'm here."

Ten gave him a bone cracking hug then regained control of her emotions. "I'm okay now. Thanks for that, Brother Thirteen. Sweet curse of the caverns, that was wild."

"Let's get you back on the ship, girl," he sighed. "Can you talk about what happened?"

"Yes. The captain will want to know, and so will Five."

She was still a bit shaky, so he steadied her as they returned to the ship to find everyone waiting. "Ten are you all right?" asked Morthel as the medic stepped toward the SUVI.

"She just needs a minute," said Thirteen as he passed her to Three who enfolded her into a motherly hug.

"Deep breaths, lock it down," soothed SUVI 3, "I've got you."

With another shuddering breath Ten straightened up, gave Three a return hug then squared her shoulders and faced the captain. "There are sentient creatures here, Captain. They're telepathic, and they're defiant, former slaves and victims. Their message was quite clear, they will not be enslaved again. They will not serve."

"There was more than that to it," said Morthel kindly as she guided Ten to a seat then sat facing her. "Can you share, or is it too personal?"

Ten sighed then nodded. "It's okay. I tried to let them know I understand; that I too was once a slave. I tried to show them a memory, but they ripped the whole thing from my mind, all the memories and the pain that went with it. It was sudden, like it was happening at that moment. It's left me a bit unsettled."

"No doubt it has," replied Morthel, giving Ten's hands a gentle squeeze.

"So, what now?" asked Commander Lilly Peters. "Is it safe for me to start gathering samples?"

"No," replied Ten, perhaps a bit too emphatically. "No, not yet," she went on, more quietly. "Sorry. I got the distinct impression they don't really want us here, and yet they do. They seem to be willing to talk but made it plain they won't help us in any way."

Lilly looked to Morthel. "Captain?"

Morthel sighed and stood up. "Thirteen, opinion please?"

"I suggest we take this one back to the admiral."

"That was my thought as well. Take us home, Three."

"Homeward bound, aye, Captain." With that the explorer ship rose from the ground and shot into space.

* * * * *

Down on the planet the Marienas watched the ship leap out into space. "Will they return, do you think, Mourana?"

"Unknown, but I believe they will. The communicator is strong, I believe she will return. We will need to study and test them thoroughly for they are strong and could prove difficult to overcome."

* * * *

The briefing room of the Reacher was filled with the captains and the admiral as well as SUVI 10. "Everyone's here, Admiral."

"Thank you, Vice-Admiral Drake. People, we've called this meeting as a result of Captain Morthel's report on the planet below. Morthel, please share your findings with the captains."

"Of course, Admiral. We approached the planet and flew a standard grid search. We found several reasonable climate sections, a somewhat breathable atmosphere, and a number of ruins. As usual, we seem to be the late comers here.

"We landed and when it appeared safe, SUVIs 10 and 13 left the ship to explore. I'll let Ten relate what she encountered and experienced there."

"Ten?"

"Yes, I was first off the ship. One of my extra SUVI abilities is an affinity for plants. I was the main surface gardener on Elysium for this reason. Yes, the planet. As soon as I stepped off the ship, I felt it, a presence, angry, defiant, and yet a bit curious.

"I approached as close as I felt I should, then sat on the ground and opened myself to the land, the life of the planet. It hit me like a blow to the head, visions, visions of cruelty, pain, fear, and rage, defiance. I screamed and broke free.

"Thirteen wanted me to return to the ship, but I wanted to try again, the more fool me. I opened myself to the experience again, begging them to go slow. They did, somewhat. Long ago another space faring species came here, built cities, ravaged the lands, enslaved the population, then eventually left. Whether they were driven out or left of their own accord I don't know.

"I tried to show them that I understood; that I too was once a slave. That's where it went to hell on me. They ripped every memory I had of Elysium, of my life there, from my mind, bringing up with it the full power of the emotions. I confess it tore me up, and I fought to break free of the connection. Thirteen got me under control enough to get me back aboard the ship."

She was trembling again at this point and the admiral was instantly beside her, enfolding her in gentle arms. "That hit you hard, my sister. Sit down now, rest. After the meeting we'll head for the mess and feed you," said Suvi-jean. She carefully deposited Ten in her chair then patted her shoulder as she resumed her pacing.

"So, people, opinions?"

"There are people there, telepathic people?" asked Captain da Silva.

"Apparently so," replied Morthel.

"Linsey, I doubt your magic with language will help us here," said Amanda. "The question we face now is, do we proceed to gather resources from that planet, or do we leave it alone?"

"I think that decision falls to SUVI 10," said Captain Baris. "We sent her down to investigate, to assess. I'd like to hear her opinion."

Ten looked up to smile at the old Captain. "Yes, Sir. In spite of what happened to me, I recommend we not give up just yet. We do need to top up our resources, and that planet could yield much that is useful.

"I think I need to go back and make contact again."

"Ten?"

"Yes, Five. I think part of the problem here is I'm not a telepath, my thought processes are alien to them, difficult for them. I got the sense that they didn't want us there, but were curious about us, nonetheless. They also didn't tell me to leave, just made it clear they wouldn't help us or serve us."

"So, you want to go back."

"Want to, no, Five, but I'm willing to try for the greater good."

"All right, but I'm going with you this time."

"No, Five, you can't. If they mess me up for a while that's no big loss to the fleet. If they mess you up, that's another matter altogether."

Jeannie sighed and patted Ten on the shoulder again. "My sister, your loss would be devastating to us all, make no mistake there. However, I gave you this assignment, so I leave it up to you. Take whoever and whatever you need but promise me you will be careful.

We can always find another source of supplies, but there's only one SUVI 10, she's irreplaceable."

Ten blushed and smiled her thanks.

"Do you want Friendship to ride shotgun on this one, Ten?" asked Linsey.

"Thank you, Captain da Silva, but no. I don't want to put Eighteen anywhere near that planet. With her abilities that could be a bad mistake. No, I'll go back with Captain Morthel and the crew of EX2. We can do this."

"May I ask, SUVI 10, just what do you hope to accomplish there?" asked Captain Sheila Singh.

"I want to learn more about them, reassure them we mean them no harm, and that we have no desire to stay, merely to partake of some of the planet's bounty, to do this in a way that is acceptable to them. I guess I want to get their permission to continue."

"You did say they didn't tell us to go away."

"They didn't invite us to stay and party either, Captain Singh. I'd like to be sure we won't have any unpleasantness as we hunt and gather. I survived that encounter, but they were tentative as I was. Should they grow angry and attack with those mental abilities, it could go badly for someone without my affinity for plant life or my SUVI strength."

"Understood, Ten. Thank you."

"All right," said Suvi-jean, "we have a plan. Meeting adjourned. Come on, Ten, let's get you to the mess and get some nourishment into you. I want you to be well fed and rested before you go back there again."

"Can't argue with that," smiled Ten. "Take me away."

Once again Soren noticed Ten in the mess, but she was sitting with the admiral and several of the captains. Slowly she screwed up her courage and began to approach. She had nearly reached the table when Commander Ebony Graves appeared and sat in the open space beside SUVI 10. Again Soren sighed and turned away.

Soren noticed several of the other Earalith at a different table; she decided to join them. The topic of conversation was about the encounter on the new planet. "What do you mean, terrorized?" she asked as she sat with them. "Who was terrorized?"

"Your girlfriend," said one, "you know, the SUVI you beat up a few days ago."

"Her? Someone terrorized *her*?"

"Some thing. Apparently, she has an affinity for plant life, and the planet has sentient plants or something like that. They're telepathic and put her through the ringer. Look, there she goes now."

Soren looked over to see the admiral leading the woman away. "Poor Ten," sighed someone.

"Ten?"

"Yes, that's her name, SUVI 10."

"Oh, I didn't know that." Soren returned her gaze to her plate, her heart going out to SUVI 10, she was all too familiar with being terrorized, she almost wished she could go to SUVI 10 and offer some comfort.

Later that night as Soren settled into bed, she thought of the woman she'd hit. "SUVI 10, I know what it feels like to be abused. Now I'm truly sorry for what happened and wish I could make it up to you. They said you're going back there; I hope you change your mind."

* * * * *

As always, the Marienas came to gaze at the sky. The thought, question, was formed in the general consciousness. "Mourana, share what you have learned."

"This I have learned of them. They are many, and of diverse groups, some once were enslavers, but no longer. The one sent to us was a former slave, and a member of one of the smaller groups. Its pain was akin to our own. This is what I learned." A blur of Ten's memories brought many groans of pain and sympathy.

"That one now serves by its own choice."

"It still serves the masters? Why?"

"There is still much to learn of this, to understand. I believe it will return and we can learn more."

"Did it convey to you what they want here?"

"Food, plants from the ground to nourish them, metals, and machines from the ruins if any might be used. Perhaps more. It is to be noted this one asked our permission to take these things."

"Which plants do they want for nourishment? They cannot have ..."

"Of course not. If, when, it returns this will be made plain. The difficulty is their inability to communicate clearly. The process is extremely slow and painstaking."

"Have you tested it?"

"Yes. This one is strong, and defiant even as we are, but can be broken if the need arises. There is more to learn here, more testing to be done. I will now share with you the results of the testing."

There was a quick hum then a response. "We believe Mourana will succeed, and we wish to learn more of them. Proceed as best you can, Mourana." With that the Marienas turned their attention to the night skies.

Round Two

Next morning the explorer ship set out for the planet once again. Ten sat by herself, breathing deeply, her eyes glowing amber. She heard Thirteen's voice behind her. "If that thing attacks her again today it's getting a taste of a blaster."

"Thank you, my brother, but I can deal with this. What I need you to do is stay beside me and pull me out if it goes crazy on me again. Don't hurt it; that'll only make things worse."

Thirteen sighed and relaxed his shoulders. "All right, Ten, I'll leave the blaster on the ship."

"I'll be on ship's guns," said his wife, Connie, the Security officer for EX2. "You come running and anything chasing you is going straight to hell in small pieces."

"I love it when you get all fierce," grinned Thirteen. Connie grinned, shook a finger at him, then mounted the gun turret.

"Ship has landed," announced SUVI 3, the ship's pilot.

With a sigh and a deep breath to steel her resolve, Ten rose to her feet. "Wish me luck." With that she stepped through the open hatch. Slowly, she walked to the place she'd been on her last visit and sat down. Breathing deeply, she placed her hands on the ground and called in her mind. "I have returned. Will you speak with me again?"

"YES," belled that voice in her mind.

Ten winced then replied. "Please speak more softly. Your voice is strong and brings me pain."

Several moments later the voice returned. "The process is difficult with one who struggles to speak," it replied more softly, yet Ten felt under great strain. "We will strive to not cause you pain. We would know more of what you seek here. Why have you come to the Marianas?"

"The Marianas, that is your people?"

"Yes. The one through which we speak is Mourana, the strongest of us, perhaps the leader as you might understand."

"Then I greet you in peace, Mourana."

"Why have your kind come here? Why have you chosen this place?"

"When you say this place, do you mean where I sit now, or the world of the Marienas?"

"Yes, the world of the Marienas. Why did you come here?"

Ten took a deep breath then began forming the words and pictures in her mind. "Our combined peoples are from far away. As we travel through space we try to learn as much as we can about the worlds we encounter. We also gather the resources we need to sustain our lives and maintain our ships, the homes that carry us.

"As we journeyed, this world became our next stop, for we need food and metals. Will you allow this?"

"You ask permission of the Marienas?"

"We do, yes. If you do not wish to share, we will leave, but we are in need and ask for your compassion."

"You will not compel us?"

"No, we will not attempt to compel you."

"What foods do you need? Can you not gather nourishment directly from the soil and sun?"

"We can, but even as soil must be nourished with decaying bodies of the once living and still alive, so must we."

"There are many that are ... precious to the Marienas. We would not want them harmed."

Ten struggled against the waves of nausea and weakness in her muscles as she spoke. "I understand. If I personally gather the samples we need, under the supervision of Mourana, will you allow this?"

"How would this be done?" Ten formed a picture in her mind of Lilly gathering samples with herself standing by. She pictured a shadow beside her directing which plants could be harvested and which not.

"This might be possible. The Marienas will consult together when the stars come out. Mourana will meet you here when next the sun returns, you will have an answer then. For now, you may investigate the ruins for whatever you might find useful."

"Thank you, Mourana, I'll inform my people. We will not disturb the plants but will investigate the ruins for useful metals. May the rains fall gently upon you until we meet again."

As Ten rose and walked unsteadily back to the ship, a startled and bemused Mourana watched from the dense foliage. "It gave us a blessing. Even though we caused it great pain, this time it gave a blessing. We must ponder this until the skies darken and the others awaken."

As Ten returned to the ship with Thirteen close by her side, she reviewed the conversation with Mourana. There was hope and a chance if she could just manage the pain of the connection. Once inside the ship she fairly collapsed in a seat, holding her head.

"Ten?" Captain Morthel's voice betrayed her concern.

"It's all right, Captain. I just need a few minutes to shake off the headache."

"Here, take this," smiled the ship's medic, holding out a small cup with a pill in it. "It'll fix you right up."

"Thank you," sighed Ten as she swallowed the pill and handed the disposable cup back to him.

"Report, Ten." The captain's voice was soft, soothing.

Ten smiled her appreciation. "We have permission to investigate the ruins and to take whatever we find useful. The Marienas will confer tonight and give us an answer about the soil and plant samples tomorrow. If they decide to allow that there will be one of them supervising the collection. It will tell me what we can and can't have, and I'll relay that to Lilly."

"That'll be a painfully slow process," sighed Commander Lilly Peters, "but better than nothing."

The captain rose from her seat and patted Lilly's shoulder. "Since we now have permission, let's go explore those ruins, see if we can find anything useful. Three, move us over closer to that open square area."

"Ship rising," came the voice from the pilot's station. The ship swept gracefully over the ruins and settled to the ground in what looked like it might have been a city square or a parking area of some kind. "Ship has landed, Captain."

"Then let's get to it. Thirteen, Connie, check it out." The hatch flew open and they stepped out, weapons drawn, and proceeded cautiously. It was a good thing they did, a monstrous predator suddenly leaped at them, but Connie brought it down with her blaster and finished it with her side arm. She winked at Thirteen then led the way toward what looked like a warehouse or other storage building.

Suddenly they were both attacked, terrible pain in their heads. Everyone on the ship heard them scream and Ten knew what it was. Fighting the fatigue in her own body, she raced outside, shouting. "Mourana, stop, you must stop."

"They ended a life of Mariena, this will not be tolerated," belled that voice in her mind.

"You must stop or all life on Mariena will end. Stop, and speak more softly. You're hurting us and the admiral will not tolerate that."

"What do you mean? Explain."

That voice tried to explore her thoughts again, but she was ready for it this time. Ten fought back with the image of Orca's weapons cutting open the stronghold of the Paraka. She then changed that to a vision of Orca razing the forests of Mariena. The voice fled her mind.

Connie and Thirteen both groaned their relief as the pain began to subside. "Go back to the ship now, get something to help with that headache."

"Ten?"

"Easy, brother, I'll stay here and try to sort this out."

"Are you sure about this?"

"I am, Connie, it'll be all right."

"Maybe," growled Thirteen, "but I'm manning the guns. I've about had my fill of these things."

SUVI 10 watched them go then sank to her knees and put her hands flat on the ground. "I know you can hear me, Mourana. We must talk, this is a time of grave danger."

"What do you mean?" The voice was softer, more tentative.

"You harmed one of our people, this will anger the admiral. Mourana, that creature tried to kill us; our people simply defended themselves. This creature is a predator, why does this disturb you so?"

"All life is in balance, any death that is premature can upset the balance we have struggled for so long to maintain. The loss of a single creature like this will put the Marienas in danger."

"Explain."

"We nurture our relationship with the predators so they will keep the plant eaters away from our gardens, our places of rest."

"Your places of rest? Explain."

"Marienas rest during the time of sunshine, drawing nourishment from the soil and sky. When the stars come out, so do we, to move about, to explore the world around us."

"So you rest in the soil and sun, but move about at night. I understand. We spoke of a bargain, you and me. You need to commune with the Marienas, and I need to report to the admiral. Shall we meet again tomorrow to further discuss this?"

"Yes." With that Mourana was gone from her mind and Ten sighed with relief. She struggled to her feet and returned to EX2.

"Ten?"

"All is well, Captain, and I've learned much. I'd like to share what I've learned with the admiral and the captains."

"Care to share with me first?"

"Forgive me, Captain Morthel, you're right, as leader of this expedition you need a report. This is what happened and what I've learned.

"The sentient people of this planet are mobile plants as far as I can understand. They sleep in the sun during the day, probably sinking roots into the soil while they do. They come out at night and move around.

"I had negotiated a partial treaty with them allowing us to explore the ruins, but we missed a vital piece of information. As mobile plants they have no fear of predators. In fact, they keep them around to control the numbers of herbivores in the area. Yes, Connie killed its pet, and it was angry."

Morthel chuckled at that. "What did you say to placate it?"

"I didn't try to placate Mourana, I tried to scare the hell out of them. I showed them Orca cutting through the metal doors of the Paraka stronghold when Five went to war with the gods, then I showed it Orca razing the forests of this planet. That got their attention.

"The original bargain I offered was we get full access to the ruins and Lilly taking her samples with me at her side relaying instructions from Mourana, you know, which plants we could harvest and which not. After this little episode I hope they'll stick to that."

"I understand and agreed, Ten. You're quite right, we do need to share this with the admiral. Three, take us home. Comms, get me the Reacher."

"Aye Captain, homeward bound." The ship rose into the air then shot out into space.

A Difficult Conversation

As EX2 rose from the planet and headed back to the Reacher, Soren was on friendship recalibrating the new sensors, making sure everything was perfect. While she worked she overheard Captain da Silva and SUVI 18 talking. She knew she shouldn't listen, but it was hard not to. She got genuinely interested at the mention of SUVI 10's name.

"I know Ten has an affinity for plants, Eighteen, but if they have language ..."

"It's tormenting you, isn't it, my love?" chuckled Eighteen. "As I understand it, they're telepathic, conversing mostly in thought pictures. Ten has managed to make contact, but ..." at that point the call came out for the meeting of the captains.

"All captains to the bridge briefing room. Passenger representatives to the bridge briefing room."

"Well, sounds like something's up somewhere. I get the feeling Ten's on her way back with a report. You'd better scoot, you can fill me in later in Simple Pleasures."

"Count on it," grinned Linsey as she fled the ship and headed toward the bridge.

Soren gathered her courage and spoke. "Eighteen, can I talk to you about something?"

Eighteen smiled gently. "Come, sit with me, Soren. What's on your mind?"

She sat and focused her gaze on her hands in her lap, trying to keep them still. "Well, I, I really don't know where to start."

"Tell me why you fear the SUVI so. The others can feel the distance from you and some of them think it's dislike, but I know it's fear. Why? Has a SUVI ever threatened you or harmed you in any way?"

"No, well, yes, but, no not really. Okay, Antha wants me to go to this living library she and Commander Graves have set up, to talk to a SUVI."

"But?"

"But the SUVI I need to talk to is right here."

"Because I'm the smallest?"

"Can't fool you, can I? Yeah, that's part of it all right. When I was a child my brother tortured me, tormented me to make me scream. Because he was male, and I was female, it was ignored. When I escaped to the colony I thought I was free of all that, but I bonded with a man who beat me whenever I didn't please him, and that was often.

"Eighteen, I've been abused all my life and I'm a scared little person. Everybody is bigger and stronger than I am, everybody could easily hurt me, especially the SUVI. You guys are all so damn strong, it scares me."

"Soren, if I've ever ..."

"No, you haven't, not ever."

"But one of us did?"

"Yes. I'm sure you heard all about it by now."

"Your close encounter in the mess hall a while ago."

"Yeah, that. The thing is, I'm still tormented about that. I've tried a few times to track her down and apologize for the way I acted, but by the time I work up my nerve, she's off with someone and ..."

"What's her name, do you know?"

"Ten. It took me a while to learn that, but her name is Ten. The thing is, now she's on that damn planet and those things are hurting her. I saw the shape she was in after that first contact. I also know she insisted on going back there. Why would she do that, Eighteen? Why go back to where they hurt you? I don't understand."

Eighteen smiled gently and patted her hand. "The needs of the herd outweigh the needs of the one."

"I still don't understand."

"We need supplies, to gather resources. The admiral would rather gain the permission of the indigenous species of a planet rather than just take what we want. Ten knows this. With her affinity for plants, she's the most likely to gain that permission, to be able to communicate with them.

"She goes back in hopes to get their permission to harvest, even though that communication will bring her pain. To a SUVI it's worth the personal pain to acquire food and resources for the herd, the people of the fleet."

"I don't understand you guys at all."

"I know, we don't either most of the time."

"But I want to, dammit. For example, why even stay on the Reacher when you were set free, even though your tormentors were here too?"

"As Five said that day, on Reacher we would be free, there would always be food and shelter, and it never rains."

She was grinning and Soren chuckled. "You guys are all crazy. Eighteen, what can you tell me about Ten? I really do want to apologize to her. I admit she scares the hell out of me, but I have to get past that."

"This is important to you, isn't it?"

"Yes, it is. I can't tell you why, but it is."

"All right, here's what I can tell you about Ten. She has an amazing affinity for plants, where they grow, how the grow, what's good to eat and what's not. On Elysium she was the main gardener above ground. She defended her gardens against all creatures, and those in the area learned to stay away from her. She always planted on the hillsides, away from a migration route.

"As a person, Ten is a bit shy at first, but a bubble of fun when you get to know her. We've only discovered this since coming to the Reacher. She's gentle with everybody because she knows her strength. Only Nineteen and Five are stronger.

"I can also tell you she's been looking for you too, wanting to apologize for scaring you. She's deeply troubled about this, but she doesn't know your name, so it's been hard for her to locate you. She's also scared she might frighten you again by just approaching you so, ..."

"Seriously? She's scared of me?"

"Of frightening you, Soren. Ten would never hurt you."

"But she could."

"Yes."

Soren let out a deep sigh then looked up. "She's really gentle?"

Eighteen grinned. "Oh girl, you have no idea. Ten will be a fierce warrior if threatened or if her people are threatened, but as a friend you'll find no one more gentle, more trustworthy, and protective than SUVI 10."

"Really?"

"Yes, really. Soren, if you're sure about trying to get past your fears of the SUVI, talk to Ten, make friends with her, get to know her. She won't be on that planet forever; she's usually working in hydroponics or in the soil gardens."

"Okay, so how do I make friends with a super SUVI?"

"Ask her about the soil gardens, Ten set those up herself. Until we SUVI came aboard, the Reacher depended solely on hydroponics. Lilly wanted to test the different soils of the different planets and Ten was all over the idea. Plants are her passion."

"Okay, that actually sounds interesting. Thanks, Eighteen."

"Any time, Soren. You can come to me any time."

"Thanks, and I know what you're doing."

"Oh?"

"You've been holding my hands, trying to show me you won't hurt me, that I'm safe with you."

"Did it work?"

That made Soren laugh. "Yes, it worked. I can't thank you enough for this."

"All my pleasure, sister Soren. We're the crew of Friendship, we need to all be friends, right? So, off you go and hunt down a SUVI."

"I'll go hang out in the mess, ambush her when she comes in," chuckled Soren.

* * * * *

"All captains and passenger representatives are here, Admiral," smiled Amanda.

"Thank you, Mandy. Morthel, report."

"Admiral, we returned to the planet where SUVI 10 was able to hammer out a possible solution for us. Under that agreement we would get full access to the ruins for salvage, and a controlled access to the plant life there.

"We approached the ruins; Thirteen and Connie were attacked by a huge predator, but Connie brought it down. That's when the Marienas attacked them. SUVI 10 managed to call the Marienas off then reported back to me.

"Admiral, I'd like to have Ten relay what happened and what she's learned."

"Agreed. Ten, my sister, what can you tell us about this place, these people?"

Ten rose and smiled shyly at the room. She looked haggard. "Admiral, captains, the people of Mariena are, as we guessed, mobile plant life. They rest in the soil and sun during the day and move about at night. They're telepathic, conversing in picture thoughts primarily. I've managed to communicate with the one that represents them, their leader.

"They were once enslaved by the species that built the cities, but those people eventually left the planet. The Marienas remained behind, living in small gardens, and moving about at night. They keep large predators close to control the herbivores, prevent them from getting into the sleeping gardens.

"When Thirteen and Connie were attacked, she killed the beast. Mourana then attacked them, causing them terrible pain in the head.

Those headaches are truly violent. I heard their cries of pain and went to them, calling out to Mourana, and convinced them to stop."

"You keep saying them, yet you speak of a single representative," said Captain Baris.

"Yes, Captain. They all speak through that one, and as far as I know, they're genderless."

"Stay on track now," chuckled Jeannie. "Tell me how you got them to stop."

"When I first bargained with them, they gave us permission to explore the ruins and take whatever we could find useful. They also agreed to confer with the rest about the possibility of a supervised gathering of plant samples.

"After Connie killed the beast and they attacked, I took off the gloves and fought back. I showed them Orca cutting through that Paraka stronghold, then I showed them Orca razing the forests and fields of Mariena. I told them if they attacked and harmed our people it would anger you and this would happen. Mourana was easier to talk to after that.

"From there I returned to EX2 and reported to Captain Morthel."

"I see," mused Jeannie. "You didn't try to placate them?"

"No, Five, I didn't. They were getting far too aggressive, so I fought back. Did I do wrong?"

"My beloved sister Ten, you did nothing wrong, and you make me proud. You defended our people successfully. They got pushy and you slapped their fingers. They'll be easier to deal with now, but first I want an honest opinion from you."

"Oh?"

"I can see the pain in you, my sister, the cost of conversing with these creatures. In your opinion, is there likely to be anything on that planet worth paying this price? I confess I'm reluctant to send you back there."

Ten looked thoughtful for a few moments then nodded. "As we flew the original grid search there were pockets of grain growing in the forests near the ruined cities. I'm certain these are remnants of once vast farms, yet the forests and Marienas themselves have been unable to overcome them completely.

"Such a hardy grain species would surely be a welcome addition to our stock if it proves up. I say it's worth another try, and if I can't get their permission we go anyway."

"Ten?"

"I don't like them, Five, they remind me too much of the masters on Elysium, aggressive, demanding, assuming complete ownership, assuming their gods given right to control ..."

"Easy, Sister Ten, easy. You've done more than enough here, risked enough, endured enough, too much. I'll go talk to them myself."

"No, Five, I'll go. I've built a small rapport with Mourana, such as it is. We need you here, at full strength. Dealing with these things is draining, draining my mind, my strength, and it will take time to recover. Should something go amiss we need you at full power, not lost in a brain fog, struggling to focus."

"There's another option," said Sessas.

"Sessas?"

"Retriever go down, Strikers carry flame throwers, protect people. They hurt our people, no longer need permission. Flame throwers keep away, we take food, leave planet."

"You make a strong point, Sessas, and I'll admit, it is appealing. Opinions? Options?"

"Give me one more shot at it, Five," said Ten as she rose to her feet again. "I can do this, I can. Let me try again."

Jeannie's shoulders sagged as she nodded. "All right, Ten, but if they hurt you again we're going in hard. Morthel, keep a close eye on her. At the first sign of trouble get her out of there."

"Understood, Admiral. I won't hesitate."

With that the meeting broke up and they headed for the mess and a meal.

* * * * *

While Ten settled into bed for a night's rest the Marienas gathered under a cloudy sky. "Mourana, what more have you learned?"

"There is much to consider. At first there was agreement, they could have the ruins and whatever useful things they could yield. They asked to gather plants for food, but agreed to be supervised, take only what was allowed. As we conferred, I increased the testing, but this one is strong. It withstood much and still managed to remain conscious.

"They moved off to inspect the ruins but were attacked by a predator. They killed it and I attacked them."

"And rightly so."

"No, that was a mistake. Their speaker came hurrying to me, commanding me to stop and explain why I had done so."

"Commanded? It dared to command you? It ..."

"Yes. Please, please stop and hear the rest. I did explain why I had done so, and it told me that attack would anger their leader. It showed me what the leader might do. I will share this with you now."

There were shrieks of fear and outrage as the images flashed through the collective minds. "Mourana, you must drive them away."

"That is no longer possible, for in the heat of the moment I made a grave error. I told that one that we rest in the soil and sun, only to move about at night, that the predators were there to keep us safe from plant eaters.

"That one speaks with difficulty, but it is intelligent. It won't take it long to find the day gardens then we are helpless, as good as dead. Forgive me, Marienas, for I have failed you."

There was a lot of fearful fussing and a flurry of ideas. "We must move the gardens."

"Sadly, my people, it is too late for that now. It knows and it will find us."

"Kill it."

"If I do their leader will send the fire breathers, the soil burners. They will raze the lands and take what they want, whatever they want, and then destroy the rest."

"Then what do we do? Mourana, what must we do?"

"The speaker appears to be reasonable. Perhaps we can still get them to agree to the original bargain, to harvest only what we want and none of our youth in the secret gardens."

"Will you continue the testing?"

"I will, for now it is even more imperative that we learn the means to break them down."

"Do it, Mourana, we will all hold you in our thoughts and will you to succeed."

Going Back Down

Soren's attempt to ambush Ten at the mess failed again as the woman was surrounded by SUVI. She was saddened by how haggard SUVI 10 looked and she already knew the Marienas had attacked the explorers and Ten had fought them off. Soren was tormented and starting to get a bit frustrated, she had to do something. Next morning as Ten left her quarters for EX2 she found a small, determined woman blocking her path.

"Stop right there, SUVI 10."

Wide eyed, Ten stopped in her tracks and knelt down so she would be looking slightly up at the smaller woman. "I've been looking for you to apologize. I'm deeply sorry I scared you so badly. I swear I'd rather die than hurt you."

Soren sighed and looked at her own shoes. "I've been trying to corner you for days, to apologize to you for my bad behavior. I hit you and yelled at you, and that was wrong. Sorry."

"Forgiven, my friend. May I know your name?"

"Huh? Oh, yes, I'm Soren."

"Soren, I'm so thrilled you tracked me down, and I'd love to waste a day or two just talking to you, but I have to go now. Can we meet in the mess when I get back? I promise to be careful where I sit."

Soren's eyes snapped up to see the small grin of mischief playing at Ten's lips, and yet the fatigue was also there. "You're teasing me about that?"

"You're right, I am, and I'm so ashamed."

"You're not either, you're laughing at me again."

"Soren, I'll admit I'm teasing you a bit, but I'm not laughing at you. I am, however, enjoying you."

With a deep sigh Soren gazed at her for a moment. "Ten, I can see the pain in your eyes; please don't go back there where they can hurt you."

Ten's expression softened and she reached to gently take Soren's hands in her own. "Thank you for that, but I have no other choice; I have to go back."

"Why? Why can't somebody else do it? Why not one of ..."

"Because I can communicate with them, nobody else can. If I don't go the admiral might send down the strikers and a lot of the Marienas will die."

"Why can't we just move on? We're not that desperate for supplies."

"Yet. Soren, the last system was barren. We're running low of a few things; if we leave and the next system proves barren then we could be in trouble. We can top up here, and we do need to. Five knows this. If I can succeed in getting the cooperation of the Marienas then there need be no loss of life. If I can't it could go ugly."

"But they're hurting you."

"It's okay, I'm tougher than I look."

"That's not the point, Ten ..."

"I know, I know, Soren, and you have no idea how much it thrills me that you care, it truly does. Tell you what; when I get back you can nurse me back to health."

Soren saw the small grin on Ten's face and squeezed the hands in hers. "Be careful what you wish for, super SUVI. I'll be waiting for that ship to come home, and you'd better be in one piece."

The comms interrupted at that point. "Thirteen to Ten, you coming or what? Ship's waiting."

"On my way. Soren, it would make my world to have you meet me when I return. I'll look forward to it all day."

"Just promise to be careful. Come back in one piece."

"I promise. Just promise we can spend a few days getting to know each other when I do."

Soren squeezed her hands again. "I promise, now scoot, Morthel will be pacing by now."

"I hear and obey," grinned Ten as she leaped to her feet and raced away.

Ten came running onto the launch bay and hurried into the ship. "Captain, so sorry, I ..."

"Got ambushed?" Suvi 10 turned to see the captain grinning at her. "It went well?"

Ten nodded. "Then I'm happy for both of you. Three, get us down onto that planet. The sooner we get to work the sooner we can get Ten home for some R&R."

Blushing, Ten stepped to the sensor panel as the small ship leaped away from the Reacher. Thirteen reached out to lightly grip her arm. She looked up and he quirked an eyebrow. At her shy smile and nod he winked and, patting her arm, turned away.

As she turned back to the screen she noticed something. "Captain, we appear to have much of the fleet along with us today."

"Oh?"

"Three ships."

"Two are the salvage ships in case we get lucky," replied Morthel.

"And the other?"

"Retriever in case we don't."

"Understood," nodded Ten. The admiral had been distressed at how haggard she'd been on her last trip, and how tired she looked this morning. Captain Sessas was along in case things went sour. There would be no holding back if the strikers got involved. She had to make Mourana understand what was at stake.

"Approaching planet, Captain."

"Thank you, Three. Ten, this is your show, where do you want to land?"

"Back to the original location if that's okay," replied Ten.

"Got it. Three?"

"Approaching desired coordinates, Captain. Ship has landed."

"Thank you, pilot. All yours Ten."

"Aye, Captain. Wish me luck."

She stepped out into the light rain with Thirteen and Connie close behind. Sinking to the ground, palms flat to the soil, she called out in her mind. "Mourana, are you there?"

The voice that sounded in her mind was softer this time, and yet there was something about it Ten didn't like. "We are here."

"My people will investigate the ruins now. Do not interfere or challenge them."

"You no longer ask permission? Now you dictate terms? We will not obey you. We will not serve."

Ten sighed then, fighting the pain in her head, formed her reply. "We do not ask you for service, nor do we issue demands or terms. Yet."

"What do you mean, yet?"

"The great admiral was angered by what happened yesterday. Today you see more ships in the skies. Two are here to investigate the ruins."

"And the other?"

"That one is here to ensure the safety of our people. Attempt to interfere with them and violence will ensue. You gave permission for us to explore and salvage among the ruins, that is what they are doing today."

"If they stay within the ruins we will not hinder them."

Ten nodded and reached for her comms. "Ten to EX2."

"Morthel here."

"Captain, it's safe for the explorers to investigate the ruins. Mourana assures me they will not be interfered with."

"Understood." A few moments later they watched as Retriever settled to the ground at the edge of the ancient city. The strikers stepped out with flame throwers and other weapons at the ready. When nothing happened the two salvage ships descended, and the investigations began.

Mourana said nothing and neither did Ten as they watched the ships land. "SUVI 10, those people want to harm the Marienas."

"Perhaps, but they won't unless they have to. It's best to avoid them. Let us now discuss the gathering of plants."

"You must be extremely careful and take only what we agree to."

"I understand. Let's begin here." She got a clear picture in her mind of the grain filled clearings in the nearby forests.

"That? That is what you want?"

"I believe it may be our best bet, at least I'd like to start there, take a few samples to study, see if it will meet our needs."

"Take what you will from that place and those like it, nothing more."

"Do you want to supervise?"

"There are no young gardened in such places. There is no need."

"Then this day we will do that and nothing more. May the gentle rains nourish the Marienas this day." With that she rose shakily and went back to the ship where the medic was waiting with headache meds for her.

"Again, even though we increased the testing, the pain we sent to it, it gives us a blessing yet moments ago it threatened us. Or did it? Perhaps it wasn't a threat, but a warning. No matter, it can have whatever it wants from the ruins and the death fields." With that thought Mourana retired to sink roots into the soil for the day.

"What's the good word, Ten?" asked the captain as Ten reached the ship.

"We have the go ahead to take whatever we want from the grain fields in the forest, nothing more. However, Commander Peters and I agreed that's our most likely chance anyway.

"At last," sighed Lilly. "Ten, it looks like that took the good out of you. Why don't you go back to the sleeping booths and catch a nap? I can deal with the samples."

"Lilly's right, Ten," agreed the captain. "You've cleared the way for us, take a rest now." Nodding her thanks, SUVI 10 retreated to the sleeping quarters and was instantly asleep.

"I don't like this, Thirteen. Those meetings with the Marienas are too hard on her."

"I agree, Captain. With any luck this will be the last one. If they stay away from the recovery ships and we get free access to the grain fields, maybe she won't have to do it again."

"I hope you're right; the admiral didn't look happy this morning."

* * * * *

While SUVI 10 succumbed to much needed sleep, the salvage crews swept into full swing. Some of the ruins contained valuable metals plus a major bonus. An entryway to a storage and information archive was found. The call was placed to the Reacher and within moments Friendship launched and shot toward the planet.

While Captain Linsey da Silva and SUVI 18 immersed themselves in the discovery of a new language and the records of life on the planet so long ago, Commander Lilly Peters of EX2 filled her crates with plant and soil samples then the explorer ship rose from the ground and returned to Reacher.

"Ten?"

"She's still sleeping, Captain. You go report to the admiral, I'll stay here until she wakes up."

"Thank you, Thirteen. I truly hope this will be the last time she has to do that. Let her rest." With that captain Morthel left the ship to seek out the admiral. She found her pacing in the bridge briefing room.

"Morthel, you're back. Report."

"Success, Admiral. SUVI 10 secured the cooperation of the Marienas in that they agreed to let the salvage crews work unhindered. They also agreed to allow the harvesting of the forest grain fields should the grain prove useful to us.

"On her own and without the supervision of the Marienas, Commander Peters took several samples of other plant life growing near the grain. She encountered no interference."

"I see Ten didn't accompany you. Is she all right?"

"After she returned from communicating with the aliens, she retired to the sleeping quarters on EX2. She was still asleep when we returned so we left her there with Thirteen to keep watch until she awakens."

"Well done, Morthel. Do you think she'll have to go back or is that all under control for now?"

"I'm unsure, Admiral. Ten can give you a better idea herself when she wakes up."

"I'm here," came a shaky voice from the doorway. Ten was there leaning heavily on Thirteen's arm.

"My god, Ten ..."

"I'm okay, Five."

"The hell you are, my sister, the hell you are. Sit down now and tell me all, and then you're off to see Carla for a full physical."

Ten nodded then spoke, her voice quiet, subdued. "I warned the Marienas to stay back from the salvage crews. They didn't like it. Took a while to convince Mourana that we weren't making demands or dictating terms. They'd already given permission. I was merely warning them to stay back so no further misunderstandings would occur.

"We went from there to the issue of the grain fields. Eventually they agreed we could have as much of that as we wanted, and they'd leave us to it. I went back to the ship, reported to Captain Morthel then caught a nap. I guess in truth I slept away much of the day."

Suvi-jean guided Ten into a seat then knelt down to take the shaking woman's hands in her own. "Tell me you don't have to go back there again."

Ten squeezed the hands in hers and smiled weakly. "That depends on what Lilly finds out about the grain. If it has what we need then we're good to go. If she wants to explore further, then I may have to go back."

Jeannie nodded thoughtfully. "Right now the only place you're going, is to the infirmary. Thirteen take her to see Carla then back to her quarters from there as needed. I'll call the others." He nodded as he gently took Ten by the arm and guided her out of the room.

"Admiral?"

"Yes?"

"You're not going to ask further permission, are you?"

"No, Morthel, I'm not."

"Good. I saw her stagger on her way back to the ship and sent Thirteen out to help, but she waved him off. I'll admit, there's something not quite right about all this. The Earalith encountered telepathic species before, but nothing like this ever happened that I'm aware of. I think I'll consult with the others, see if anyone else has any knowledge of this sort of thing to share."

"Do it, Morthel. I'm going to check in with Twenty, get her take on it."

* * * * *

SUVI 10 didn't have a chance to go back to her quarters, the chief medical officer put her in a bed and sedated her. "I want her watched around the clock."

"Yes ma'am," replied the attendant as she settled in with the monitor.

Carla nodded and headed for her office where she found Suvi-jean waiting for her. "Jeannie, whatever the hell is going on down on that planet is killing her. I want it stopped. If I have to I'll pull rank and ..."

"No, my fierce Chief of Medical, that won't be necessary, I'm in full agreement with you. How is she?"

"She's in bad shape, Jeannie, but she's strong, SUVI strong, she'll be fine with a month or two of rest. She's sleeping now and she's being watched constantly. When she wakes up, I'll give her a dose of vitamins then send her to the mess to top up her tank, but I don't want her doing whatever it is she's doing that's causing this."

"What she's doing is interacting with a telepathic species of mobile plant."

"Really?"

"Yes, as crazy as it sounds, that's what she's doing. It's her affinity for plants that make it possible for her to communicate with them, but it drains her."

"Yes, and that mental drain is manifesting physically. It has to stop."

"Yes, Ma'am. I'll call a meeting of the captains and we'll hash out a plan of action that doesn't include sacrificing a SUVI."

Making Plans

The day was well along, and the night shift was waking up before the salvage ships and Friendship returned. Retriever was the last to settle to the deck of the Reacher. A moment later the captains were informed there would be a full meeting a 0:800 the next morning. With that the tired crews went to their beds to grab what rest they could.

Soren searched for SUVI 10 but couldn't find her. Finally she checked with the main computer. "Computer, locate SUVI 10."

"SUVI 10 is in the infirmary."

Soren raced away only to be informed that Ten was sleeping comfortably. With a sigh and mixed emotions, she returned to her own quarters for some rest. As she settled down for the night, she was relieved to know Ten was okay, but also disturbed to realize how bad she must have been to be taken to the infirmary.

She sighed deeply as she reviewed the conversation they'd had that morning. She'd felt no resentment from the woman, no threat, nor any sense of superiority from her. Instead, Ten had knelt down to be at eye level with her. She also felt a strong sense of fun from this mighty SUVI, fun and compassion. "You know, it wouldn't hurt for somebody as small as I am to have a super SUVI for a friend," she mused. "I hope the admiral doesn't let her go back down there again."

* * * * *

Morning arrived and the meeting was convened. "Looks like we're all here, Admiral."

"Thank you, Vice-Admiral. All right, people, we're here to do a bit of brainstorming. First things first, Olga, report."

"We've found a number of useful things down on the planet, Admiral. We'll be able to top up our rare metals and more. There's a lot of tech, the engineers are going over that now and with luck there'll be good things for us there as well. On top of that we discovered an old archive or library of some sort. We called Captain da Silva and gave her that one to explore."

"Excellent. Linsey?"

"It is definitely an archive of knowledge, Admiral. The Gorthas were meticulous about keeping records. We managed to get the language into the database and started poking through it."

"Have you learned anything interesting?"

"Just some impressions at this point. I know SUVI 10 has learned the current occupants of the planet were once enslaved to the Gorthas who eventually left the planet. Rather, I should say, fled the planet."

"Fled?"

"Yes, that was the translation. As near as I can guess at this point, they didn't leave willingly but were driven away."

"I see. Morthel, any word from Lilly about the grain?"

"I'll ask her, Admiral. Morthel to Lilly."

"Here, Captain."

"Any word about the grain yet?"

"Sorry, not yet. I can give you a firm yes or no in a couple of days, but ..."

"Understood, Lilly. Thank you. Morthel out."

"Well, there we have it, people," sighed Jeannie. "We'll give Lilly three days. Keep at the salvage for now, but we'll hold off on the plant life until Lilly is ready."

"Are there any further developments from SUVI 10?" asked Shiela Singh.

"And that brings me to the issue of the day. After her last round of negotiations with the Marienas, SUVI 10 was taken to medical and remains there at this time. She's the only one of us capable of communicating with them, but it's killing her to do it. Furthermore, what she reports is a people with a serious attitude problem.

"Captain Morthel informs me the Earalith encountered telepathic species before without this issue. Morthel, have you learned anything further about this?"

"Nothing further, Admiral, but I did speak with the captain of Friendship and asked her to check Ship's records, see if he had anything more to offer."

"Linsey?"

"Ship said he'd encountered three telepathic species, Admiral. The issue of pain and extreme fatigue did not manifest."

"I see."

"Admiral, what are you thinking of doing here?" asked Captain Baris of Recovery Two.

"Nothing at this time, Grandfather, but soon. First I want to get Lilly's take on it, is this worth further risk or not, and I want Linsey to delve into those archives, learn what she can about what happened here between the Gorthas and the Marienas."

"And if Lilly says we need the grain? Do we just take it?"

"After what SUVI 10 has suffered to get us this far I have to say yes. If that grain is a viable food source, I'll declare the Marienas a hostile species who attacked our envoy of peace. There will be no further negotiations. We take what we need from here then move on."

"So we'll go to war?"

"No, Grandfather. I won't hunt them as I did the Paraka, but we will take what we need and defend our people as they hunt and gather. If the Marienas come at us they pay the price, if they leave us in peace, we will do the same for them."

At that he nodded and didn't speak further. Frank Baris wasn't trying to push his granddaughter; he just wanted her to be clear on her own motives. The fleet needed supplies and what they needed was right at hand. It was now a matter of motivation, but he should have known, a SUVI would never deliberately go looking for a fight if there was another way to achieve the goal.

* * * * *

Next morning the crews gathered in the mess for a meal before heading back to their ships. As Soren sat with her tray the captain of EX2 sat across from her. "Morthel?"

"I was just at the infirmary," grinned Morthel. "Somebody was awake and aware you'd tried to visit her last night. She sent you a message."

"Oh?"

"Yes. When informed your ship had been on the surface and that it might return there today, she became distressed. She says to be careful and stay inside the ship if at all possible."

Soren sighed and nodded. "I should go see her. We should have time ..." Then the ship's comm system spoke.

"All Friendship crew to the ship, repeat, all Friendship crew to the ship."

"Aw crap."

Morthel chuckled at that. "Relax my friend, we'll be on the Reacher for the next few days until Lilly delivers her verdict. I'll take a message to Ten for you."

"Just tell her I'm sorry I didn't get to see her and to rest up until I get back." With that Soren raced away toward the launch bay.

She arrived at the ship just ahead of SUVI 18. "Soren, I was just visiting our mutual friend in medical. She said to tell you she'll be waiting for you in the mess when we get back, but I doubt Carla will turn her loose before tomorrow."

Soren nodded. "By all the spirits I hope she doesn't go back there again. It's killing her."

"Yes, it is, but she'll never admit it. Between you and me, I doubt the admiral will let her go back. She's not happy about this at all. That's what we're doing today, Linsey will be searching through those archives for any hint of what's going on and how to stop it. If we find nothing Five will stop it the hard way."

"Good, it's about time." Soren stopped and sighed. "I guess I still don't fully understand."

"Understand?"

"What drives a SUVI. After the first time they attacked Ten we should have just taken what we need."

"In truth, the admiral was ready to do just that, but Ten wanted to go back."

"Why? Why go back where they can hurt you? I know, I know, for the greater good, the needs of the many outweigh the needs of the few. But ..."

"Keep going. You're almost there, keep going."

Soren thought for a moment then sighed again. "She tried to save as many as possible of the Marienas and still get what we need. For the good of the many, all the many, both friend and foe alike. Right?"

Eighteen smiled and nodded. "Yep, that was quite probably why she insisted on going back. I truly doubt the admiral will let her go again."

"I sure hope not."

"Ship has landed, Captain Linsey," came the voice of the pilot.

"Great. Okay Eighteen, here we go. Ettlan, once we're inside, use the ship to block the entrance and keep the guns warmed up, shields raised. We're taking no chances here."

As soon as Linsey and Eighteen disappeared into the ancient structure, the ship rose from the ground, turned, then settled back down. The shields went up and Menaldo manned the guns. They settled down to wait. The day was gone and darkness falling before Linsey called for transport back to the Friendship.

* * * * *

While Linsey and crew were heading down to the planet, Ebony Graves welcomed her first visitor to the living library. "Welcome. Please have a seat. It was a Morar you requested, correct?"

"Yes, a Morar."

"Relax, have some tea; it won't be a moment." With that she walked away and a Morar in uniform soon arrived and sat down then poured himself a mug of tea. "Greetings, I am Sha'tak."

"Denny, Orca crew. Correct me if I'm wrong, but I think we've met before."

"We did, Denny; it was a fine tussle, but it got a bit out of hand."

"Yeah, Issak pulled a knife on Rayla Mills. It went all to hell from there. Look, about that tussle, as you called it. I know I was the cause of much of that and I want to apologize for it."

"Want to or was commanded to?"

Denny laughed at that. "A bit of both, I guess. No, want to. I ran my mouth instead of my brain, let the other guys egg me on, made a fool of myself, got my ass kicked, and I'm sorry for all of it."

"Don't be, my friend. It's always this way between the warriors of different clans."

"Yeah, I guess, but we need to stop that and wise up, watch each other's backs. There's only a few of us left, any of us, and we need to stick together."

"Won't argue that. Denny, why did you come here, and why ask to speak with a Morar?"

"Like I said, I messed up, and quite recently had that pointed out to me the hard way."

"Oh?"

"Yeah, a sad story for a later time. Why a Morar? I guess because I just don't understand you guys at all. You had your own planet, a home that you could survive and thrive on, but you were hell bent on joining the Wanderers. Why would you do that?"

Sha'tak chuckled at that and brushed the fur back from his eyes. "Probably for the same reasons you did."

"What does that mean?"

"You're a warrior, not a chieftain; so am I. Our clan was the defender of the sacred ship, that which brought the people away from the dealers of death to a place where we could live and grow strong. We basically worshipped the ancestors.

"Suddenly there was Captain Ka'Ron, a living ancestor, getting the elder priest and the chieftain all excited about taking the sacred ship back to the stars. The chieftain said we go, and so we came. They didn't consult me. Were you consulted before your people fled to the stars?"

"Me? Oh hell no. I'm just a grunt, I go where the captain takes the ship. No, I didn't get a vote either. You ever wish you'd stayed behind?"

"No, not really. My clan is small, and war had broken out. Even if I'd managed to survive, we'd have been absorbed into another clan, reduced in status, that sort of thing. No, on the ground I carried a spear, on the Kreenon I work the guns, same job, different place. It's not so bad here, and it never rains."

This time Denny laughed. "Yeah, I get that. For me, if I'd stayed behind, I'd have died when the home planet was wiped clean of life. I got lucky, my parents were ship's crew, I was born on a ship, grew up and became part of a ship's crew. This is all I've ever known, but I get what you mean, we go where the leaders take us and try to survive.

"So here we are, floating through the void. This is my life, always has been, but not you. This has to be harder on you. Is there anything you miss about the home world more than any other?"

Sha'tak sighed. "Mop'tar."

"What's Mop'tar?"

"A puzzle of sorts. The chieftain hides something of value in the forest, three warriors go with her. When they return, they each give a different clue to one of us. The four chosen have to work together to find what was hidden. Working alone you don't have a hope, but together it is possible. Sometimes it would take days." He was smiling as he spoke, lost in a fond memory.

Denny nodded then grinned. "That gives me an idea. We could blend that tradition with one from my people, the obstacle course. We could get a SUVI to set one up. A SUVI might be able to complete it alone, but we could never do it, we'd need to work together to complete it."

"Sounds like fun and good exercise. Do you think the SUVI will help?"

"Trust me, I know a guy. I'm sure he'll go for it. I'll check into it and message you about my progress."

"I'd like that. Thank you, my friend. Is there anything I can do for you?"

"Just don't drop me on my ass if you have to boost me over a wall."

Sha'tak laughed at that. "Agreed. I have to go now; my shift starts soon. I'll be watching for that message."

Denny watched him go with a sad look. "You know, he's not a bad sort at all, a lot like me really. I guess this is worse for him, he was dragged away from home by his chieftain, this is all the home I've ever really known." He walked away still mulling over the encounter.

As he walked out Denny noticed SUVI 19 at another table, gesturing with his hands as he spoke and a small Maccay woman busily taking notes. He winked at Nineteen as he walked by. "I'll bet Nineteen could design an obstacle course hard enough to challenge a team."

* * * * *

While Soren was getting bored on the planet and the living library was getting under way on the Reacher, SUVI 10 was getting cleared to return to quarters. The admiral and SUVI 2 met her as she left the infirmary. "Well, you're looking a lot better today."

"Thanks, Five, I'm feeling a lot better."

"Headed for the mess?"

"Yes, the mess and a taste of revenge."

"Revenge?"

"Yes, Two, revenge. I'm going for the biggest veggie burger the chef can materialize. It's payback time."

Jeannie and Two chuckled at that. "At least your sense of humor has healed. I was quite worried about you."

"I know, and I'm sorry about that, Five. I just don't understand it, that communication is all mental pictures and a few words they've managed to grasp. It shouldn't take the good out of me like that, but it does."

"I know, and the Earalith agree. They've encountered other telepaths before without this result. Linsey's going through the archives on the planet now, trying to see if she can learn anything about this. Is there anything you can tell me about that contact, anything at all?"

"As I said, it's mostly pictures and a few words, but it requires intense focus. I believe it's because our species are so utterly different."

"Do you think it affects them the same way?"

"No, I don't. They're such confusing creatures, they want to know all about us, but they don't want us near them either. However, they let it slip that they move around at night and sink roots into the soil during the day. They keep savage predators around to keep the herbivores away, and they have young growing in gardens somewhere. That's why they wanted to supervise the taking of soil and plant samples.

"When I asked about the grain fields in the forest, they called them the fields of death and said to take what we want, there are no gardens of the young anywhere near those fields."

"Hmm, that is interesting. Now, here we are, you sit to rest, and I'll see if chef can muster three veggie burgers for us."

* * * * *

While Ten enjoyed her vengeance burger, as she called it, Soren quietly nibbled on a ration bar while staring at the sensor panel. "What's on your mind?" asked the voice of her friend, Tagora.

"Huh? Oh, nothing really."

"Right, and I'm over two meters tall."

Soren chuckled at that. "Okay, I'll talk. It's Ten, I can't get her out of my mind, and I don't understand why. Why do I care so much?"

"Because she reminds you of you? She keeps going back where she'll get hurt, and she knows that but does it anyway?"

"Yeah, I guess that could be it. But it's different for her."

"Oh?"

"She told me she does it for the greater good. The fleet needs resources, we can get that here. When I said we should just take it, she said too many would die."

"Are the Marienas that much of a threat?"

"No, she said they aren't, but they're a unique species and I know she does it to keep the admiral from ordering something that would put us in danger and cause a lot of the Marienas to get killed."

"And you don't understand why she would allow herself to be hurt to protect those who hurt her."

"No, she's SUVI, for the greater good, that's why she'll do it and keep it up as long as she can."

"Okay, so what is it that has you so flummoxed?"

"Why do I care so much? I mean that. I just met her, was scared to death of her, and now I'm worried sick about her. Why?"

"Wow, when did this happen? When did you go from being scared to death to being all protective of her?"

Soren sighed and thought for a moment. "I guess it was the day I talked to her. I'd been trying to get to see her and apologize for hitting her, for yelling at her, but something or somebody always got in the way. I finally waited outside her quarters and cornered her. I guess that's when it happened."

"Tell me."

"I was still pretty scared but determined. She saw that at a glance and knelt down so she was looking up at me a bit. She listened and then apologized again for scaring me in the mess. She confessed she'd been looking for me too.

"Taggie, I could see the toll that contact with the Marienas was taking on her and begged her not to go back again. She was so sweet to me and explained why she had to try one more time. I promised to meet her when her ship got back, but we were called out and I wasn't there. When I got back, she was in the infirmary.

"Those damned Marienas are killing her, and I'm terrified she'll try to go back there again."

"And that's what's got you messed up, isn't it? You do care. The woman you met in the corridor wasn't so fierce and scary, she was a wounded soul, just like you. She got your maternal instincts going, didn't she?"

"Yeah, that and something more. I can't put my finger on it, but what I do know is I want to spend more time with her."

Tagora grinned at her and patted her hand. "You need to get your mind off this for a while. Let's check the sensors, see how many small critters we can find."

* * * * *

While Soren and Tagora hunted for small creatures on sensors, the admiral called a meeting of the captains. "Everybody's here who isn't out on a mission, Admiral."

"Thank you, Vice-Admiral. All right people, here's the latest from the planet. At the moment we have Linsey going through the archives that were found, and the recovery ships are busy at salvage. However, there is more we know of the Marienas.

"SUVI 10 reports that the Marienas sleep in gardens by day to soak up sun and moisture from the soil. They move around at night.

They also have young in special gardens. We know they keep predators around to discourage herbivores, we know they're telepathic, and we believe they're deliberately harming Ten when she talks to them.

"Each time she converses with them she suffers great pain and is physically drained by the encounter. The Earalith have encountered other telepathic species before without this problem. I now believe what is happening is deliberate on their part, for Linsey has discovered that the Gorthas were driven from this planet, they didn't go willingly."

"I don't like the sound of that," mused Sheila Singh. "What's our next move?"

"We prepare. Captains Morthel and Commander White, I'm temporarily robbing your crews for a special mission. I'm sending out the SUVI hunters to find those day gardens and map their locations. Any more trouble from the Marienas and we'll demonstrate why this is such a bad idea. Captain Sessas, keep your strikers ready, you'll fly shotgun on this one."

Jeannie reached for her comm. "Sorenson to SUVI 9, warm her up, you're going hunting. You'll have extra crew with you. I'll meet you at the ship with the mission specs."

"All right, folks, that's where we stand now. I'll keep you informed as things progress."

Jeannie arrived at the ship to find the crew ready, SUVIs Two, Twelve, and Thirteen were there as well. "All right, people, here's what I want. The Marienas are proving themselves to be difficult if not downright aggressive, but we know they move around at night and sleep in secluded gardens near the ruins by day. Nine, your specialty is finding hidden places. Find those damned gardens, log the locations, then get back here. The rest of you keep the Marienas and their pet predators off him so he can work."

"Got it, Five. Six, you'll hold the ship while I go play. Keep those guns warmed up just in case. Five, I see the crew of Retriever coming. They flying shotgun?"

"Yes indeed."

"Works for me," chuckled Nine. "Let's go hunting for gardens, family."

As they stepped onto the ship and locked the hatch Nine spoke again. "Thirteen, you've been down there, where do we start?"

"There are plenty of well used paths around and through the ruins."

"Then we start there."

Discoveries

While the SUVI went hunting for secret gardens, Soren was busy on Friendship. "Soren, what are you doing?"

"Huh? Oh playing a hunch, Taggie."

"Care to share?"

"Sure. I'm reconfiguring the sensors to pick up movement, any movement. See here, that's the crew of F1, hunting for the hiding places of the Marienas."

"Okay, so what do you suppose that shadow is?"

"I think it's one of the Marienas, damn them to the nine hells. If I can fine tune this a bit we can ... there, got you, you skeevy bastards."

That made Tagora laugh. "Soren, such language."

"Oops, sorry."

"You're not, but that's okay, you've got it. Look, we can see that thing following them. Tagora of Friendship to SUVI hunters. SUVI hunters, please respond."

"Nine, here, Tagora. What's up?"

"Nine, Soren has managed to reconfigure our sensors to see the Marienas. You've got two of them right behind you."

"Are you sure? I can't see anything, but I am getting a headache."

"Dead sure. See that rock outcrop right ahead."

"I see it."

"When your tail is right beside it, I'll alert you. If you're quick you can hit it with a blaster."

"I'd love to return some of Ten's pain to them. Just give the word."

"Stay tuned. Here they come ... now!"

At that signal SUVI Nine spun around and fired his blaster. There was a loud squeal of pain and something akin to a tree trunk appeared, tumbling over and over. "Got him, Tagora. Any more?"

"Soren?"

"Another one on your left, two meters ahead and to the left."

"Nine?"

"Got it." Another shot from the blaster and another figure tumbled away. "Any more?"

"Soren?"

"No, they're running. About twenty meters ahead there are dozens moving away from the SUVI."

"You hear that, Nine?"

"Got it. You Earalith ladies are amazing. Keep watch over the poor old SUVI while we hunt, would you?"

"Indeed we will," chuckled Tagora. "We're quite fond of the SUVI, we wouldn't want to lose any of you guys. We'll let you know if any more of them show up."

Ettlan was watching them and grinning. "Once again Earalithian ingenuity proves the equal of SUVI superpowers. I'll contact F1 and send those sensor adjustments over."

The F1 crew finished their hunt and map exercise without any further interference. As they lifted off on the return trip to Reacher, Captain da Silva and SUVI 18 called for transport out. "I think I've got enough for a report to the admiral," sighed Linsey as they reappeared aboard Friendship. "Anything exciting happen here while we were gone?"

Tagora gave her a report on the adventures with the sensors and the SUVI hunters. "Wow, Soren, well done, girl."

"Thank you, Captain."

"Come on, family, let's get back to Reacher; I have a report to make, and Soren needs some R&R time." Linsey winked at Soren as she took her seat and the agile ship leaped skyward.

* * * * *

By the time the ship arrived on the Reacher Linsey had already contacted the admiral who called a meeting of the captains and passenger reps. "Looks like everybody's here, Admiral."

"Thank you, Vice-Admiral. All right folks, Captain da Silva tells me she has much to share with us about the Marienas. Linsey."

"Yes, Admiral. I've been going through that archive that Captain Baris found. It's not so much an archive as it is a series of logs left by the scientists of the Gorthas, a record of their work, as it were. It took a while, but I found the logs pertinent to our situation. Here's what I learned.

"The Marienas were developed by the Gorthas to aid them in their farming. It was a contentious development, but they did it anyway. It was only after the Marienas gained freedom of movement that it was discovered they were intelligent, and angry, bitter, resentful. Apparently, the process that brought them from plants successful against weeds and disease to mobile beings was extremely painful for them.

"The Marienas came to understand the process that was painful, and the culled deaths of those who were unable to withstand the enforced changes. The scientists who performed the process called it testing, keeping the strong, culling the weak.

"It took several deaths in the scientific community to realize the Marienas were telepathic, and they had begun testing the Gorthas. Long story short, the Gorthas fled the planet, but not until after their number had been reduced by over sixty per cent.

"This is also interesting. The only place of refuge the Gorthas could find was in the fields of grain. The grain has a strong resistance to a certain weed, and apparently, the Marienas were developed from a variant of that weed. As well, it was the grain the Gorthas wanted the Marienas to work with, and the Marienas wanted nothing to do with it."

Jeannie paced around for a few moments. "So you're telling us those creatures were testing Ten?"

"That's what they called it. At the end, shortly before the Gorthas fled the planet, a few of them were able to communicate with the

Marienas. They tried to find a way to stop the war, but failed, it appears the Marienas enjoy the testing of other species."

"Your conclusions?"

"Admiral, I believe we're out of my area of expertise now, but I'd say the Gorthas tried to improve something, and it got away from them. Had they managed to get it right the Marienas would have had much of the planet under their control, and the Gorthas would have enjoyed the cities."

"Have you shared any of this with the folks in Hydroponics?"

"I sent some of the more technical stuff to Commander Peters of EX2 yesterday. She might know more."

"Captain Morthel."

"She's on her way, Admiral."

A moment later Lilly tapped on the door. "Enter, Lilly."

"You sent for me, Admiral?"

"I did, Lilly. Have you had a chance to look at the information Linsey sent you?"

"Yes, Ma'am, I have. I expect the original idea came from a desire to eliminate labor in the fields, to have plants themselves do it. Some of the modifications they made had unusual effects. As a result, the Marienas can emit high pitched sounds, far too high for a human to hear, but the sounds will affect us anyway."

"You mean the headaches?"

"Yes, that, and more. It appears they also emit a poisonous pheromone. One that will cause serious breakdowns in our recovery systems. I'm amazed SUVI 10 has recovered as well as she has.

"On a brighter note, that grain is a winner. I'd like to harvest as much of it as possible."

Jeannie nodded thoughtfully. "Have you shared any of this with medical?"

"Yes, Commander Marks is working on the problem now."

"Thank you, Lilly, that's great work. Sorenson to Chief of Medical."

"Here, Admiral."

"Lilly Peters has shared some info with you about the Marienas, what's the good word?"

"It is a good word, Admiral. The word is success. With this new information Dr. Reilly was able to devise an antidote and has given it to SUVI 10. She's looking better already."

"Good to know. Thank you, Carla. Sorenson out. All right, now for my end. I sent the SUVI down to find and log the location of those day gardens where the Marienas rest. SUVI 9 is here now. Nine, report."

"Success, Admiral. We located the gardens easily enough, but there were a few issues, and we began to get headaches. That's when the crew of Friendship stepped in to save us. It seems that while Friendship's captain was busy in the archives, the crew had time on their hands.

"Soren managed to reconfigure their sensors to locate and track the Marienas. We had two almost on us but were unable to see or hear them. We were getting headaches when Tagora contacted us, told us what was happening, and with their direction we were able to demonstrate the effects of a blaster. A Mariena looks much like a tree stump, can't fly worth a damn."

"Soren and Tagora. Linsey, did you know of this?"

"Yes, Admiral. They gave me a full report on the way home. F1 and the rest of the fleet now have the new sensor configuration. They can't hide from us any longer."

"Now that is good to know. It seems that we need a new kind of armor for dealing with the Marienas. Something with stronger breathing filters and hearing protection for the higher reaches of sound."

"I'll get Harlan to work on it right now," smiled Captain Moore of the Reacher as she swiftly rose to her feet. "Lilly has all the specks he'll need?"

"She does," replied Captain Morthel.

"Then with your permission, Admiral."

"Go, Rhonda. The sooner we get that armor the sooner we can harvest what we need."

* * * * *

While the meeting was convened in the briefing room, Soren went hunting for SUVI 10. She found her in the soil gardens. Soren entered the gardens but saw nothing as the plants were too high and thick for her to see over. She called out instead. "Hello the gardens, anybody home?"

"Soren, over here," replied the voice of Ten.

"Where the heck is over here; I can't see a thing over all this foliage."

That made Ten laugh. "Stay there, I'll come get you." A moment later she appeared and reached for Soren.

Wide eyed, Soren stepped into those welcoming arms and hugged her. "Wow, you're looking a lot better."

Ten smiled as she released the smaller woman from the gentle hug. "Yes, apparently your captain learned what the Marienas were doing to me and sent the specs to the chief medical officer. She passed the information to Dr. Reilly, and he came up with an antidote of sorts. Carla says I have to take it easy for a few weeks to get back to full strength, but I am feeling a lot better.

"So, enough about me, tell me of your adventures on the planet."

"Boring, Ten, at least the first couple of times. The captain went into the archives, and we set the ship to stand guard, but nothing really happened. This time the admiral sent F1 to find the day gardens and map the locations. The Marienas tried to give the SUVI headaches, but it didn't happen."

"Oh? Why not?"

"Because I found the rotten sons of Baleran. I reconfigured the sensors until I was able to see them, using the mind control to hide themselves from the SUVI. Fine, but mind tricks won't hide you from good sensor tech. As soon as I spotted them Tagora called SUVI 9 on comms, relayed the locations, and Nine hit them with blaster fire. That put a stop to their testing."

"Testing?"

"Yes. Apparently, they like to test other species, see how much they can take before they crack or crash physically. That's what they were doing to you. There were probably several of them all around you while you talked with that one. I'd like to ..."

"Oh dear god, you're so fierce," breathed Ten as she hugged Soren again. "You did that for me, didn't you?"

"Yes I did," sniffed Soren as she buried her face against the taller woman's shoulder. "They were hurting you, terrorizing you, and I know what that feels like."

"Tell me," whispered Ten as she held the smaller woman gently and kissed her hair. "Tell me all of it."

For some reason Soren could not name, she did. Suddenly, in the arms of a super SUVI, the dam burst, and she sobbed out the whole tale of her life being tormented and abused by those more powerful that she.

"Never again," whispered Ten. "You've got a SUVI for a friend now and I won't let anyone hurt you again, ever."

Soren sniffed again and began to untangle herself from Ten's arms. "Ten, I'm so sorry, I didn't mean to ..."

"Hush now, you've held much of that inside for too long. Never again, I promise. We'll hang out together so everybody can see you've got a protector. Okay?"

"Sure, okay, yeah, I'd like that. It's strange, Ten, I was so scared of you at first, but ..."

"After you beat me up you felt safe knowing I'm a ..."

"A sweet nut," giggled Soren, "that's what you are. Now stop this and show me this amazing garden. Eighteen says it was all your idea and that you made it yourself."

"It was and I did," smiled Ten as she released Soren from her arms but continued to hold her hand. "Lilly wanted to see how some plants would respond to different soils from different planets. We're using these cabbages as test plants. This area is from soil taken from Frigid where we found you. Over here is soil from IGEN, and here we have soil from old Earth mixed with the soil of Elysium and Frigid."

She went on to give the full tour all the while holding Soren's hand. For some reason she couldn't understand, Soren enjoyed the connection and stepped closer. She knew how powerful this SUVI could be, and it felt safe to be close to her, to be protected.

Eventually they headed for the mess where they were instantly greeted by a call from SUVI 9. "Ten, it's about time you two surfaced. Join us, I need your help."

Somewhat perplexed, Ten and Soren selected a meal then joined their friends. "Okay, Nine, what's up?" asked Ten as she carefully seated Soren then sat beside her.

SUVI 9 chuckled as he motioned to Tagora who sat near him. "I've been trying to recruit Tagora and Soren for F1 crew. These women are magic."

"Can't argue that. So, how's it working out for you?"

"Ten, I'm in trouble. Eighteen has threatened to cuss me out in seven different languages if I steal any of her magic crew. Help me here."

"Sorry brother, but there's no way I'll risk the wrath of Eighteen."

"You're a wise woman, my sister," chuckled Eighteen. "I see you're on the mend."

"I am. Once Commander Marks had those specs, she and Dr. Reilly worked up a fix for me. So, Soren says the Marienas were testing me, seeing how much I could take, is that right?"

"It is," replied Lilly Peters as she joined them at the table. "Want some payback?"

"Oh, you know I do."

"Oh no you don't."

"Soren?"

"You're still not fully recovered. I'm not letting you go back there until ..."

"Whoa, down girl," chuckled Lilly. "That's not what I meant. The admiral has Harlan working on a special armor just for this planet, something to block the Marienas. I want Ten to help me figure out a possible herbicide to hit them with just in case it all goes truly nasty."

"Oh, sorry."

"Don't be," smiled Ten as she patted Soren's hand. "I like it, my fierce warrior woman."

"Soren, you're the one who worked out the sensors so we could detect them, is that right?" asked Lilly.

"Yes. I really wanted to find those nasty ..."

"EX2 could use a good sensor tech."

"Forget that, Commander Peters," said SUVI 9. "F1 has a prior claim."

Eighteen shook a finger at both of them. "That's it. Any more attempts to steal my crew and there'll be trouble, and the two of you'll be in it."

There was laughter all round at that and Soren sighed to realize the SUVI were something quite different from any species she'd ever met. They were all super powered in one way or another, but they all seemed to be focused on a single goal, blend in and be accepted by everyone else, to be part of the herd. It was easy to see once you understood them better.

It was also clear none of them would ever hurt anyone else deliberately. She shifted slightly closer to Ten and felt truly safe for the first time she could remember.

The Course

SUVI 19 sat back and grinned at the man across the table. "Let me get this straight, you want me to devise an obstacle course that only a SUVI might be able to complete, is that right?"

Denny grinned and nodded. "Yep, that's right. Make it hard for a SUVI so it will take two or three others working together to complete it." Seeing the raised eyebrow, he sighed. "All right, I'll talk. I went to the living library like you said. They actually paired me up with the Morar I wrestled with in that brawl where Issak got his arm broken.

"Anyway, while we were talking, Sha'tak said he really missed a game they played on his home world. In the game the chieftain would hide something in the forest, and it would take a team of four working together to find it. I thought the obstacle course would be close enough, you know, if it took three or four of us to make it through. You know, fun, friendly interspecies relations, and good training at the same time. What do you think?"

Nineteen chuckled. "I love it, Denny, but I'll need some help with this one. Give me a couple of days and I'll get back to you." He rose to go then stopped. "I'm proud of you for this one, Denny, I truly am."

Three days later Sha'tak returned to his quarters aboard the Kreenon to find the message on his personal computer. "Hey there, it's Denny. That obstacle course is in the works. It'll take four of us to complete it, you, me, a Maccay and an Earalith. You see if you can recruit a Maccay and I'll hunt up an Earalith. Good luck."

Sha'tak brushed the fur back from his eyes and smiled. This could be fun. "I'll bet Mesera would be up for it," he mused as he left the quarters in search of a possible ally. "She's Chief of Security and quite an athlete. I'll go run it by her."

He found her in the mess aboard the Kreenon. It seemed off to him that a pacifist Maccay had been chosen as security chief, but her natural take charge manner and athleticism had swiftly earned the respect of the Morar. Smoothing the fur on his chin he approached.

Mesera had been lost in thought, daydreaming of a small man with a delightful sense of humor and two thumbs on each hand. She'd met Menaldo in the mess aboard the Reacher and had taken to him instantly. As an Earalith he was a normal size, not one of these oversized humans or SUVI. He'd been all over that vast empire before being trapped on that frozen planet, and he had such wonderful stories to tell.

She looked up as Sha'Tak approached, a bit miffed at being interrupted in her delightful fantasy. "Something I can help you with, Gunner?"

"Yes, Mesera, there actually is. Listen to this. I volunteered for that living library aboard the Reacher."

She listened politely as he related how he had met Denny and what was happening. He wanted her to sign on as part of his team, and she was about to say no when his communicator buzzed. Denny had recruited Menaldo for their team, Mesera signed on. This was a chance too good to miss.

While Sha'tak and Denny worked on recruiting a team, another team was hard at work, brainstorming. Nineteen had gone to Rayla Mills for help to design the course, then called in Ebony Graves to help with the rest. Ebony had acquired space in the passenger's area and a number of former colonists to do the building. To everybody's surprise, Ebony had asked Edran to help with the design.

The obstacle course was being built, yet Nineteen wasn't as happy as he should be about it. He'd succeeded at the task of getting the crew hardheads to change the way they saw the world and their place in it. The problem? The problem was the damned SUVI mating instinct. For some reason he couldn't name that Maccay woman had lit him up and he craved more of her company. Sadly, she'd spoken of a husband. Ah well, he'd just have to accept whatever time with her he could get.

For her part, Leela was as surprised as Nineteen. His sheer size and reputed strength were somewhat intimidating, but he'd been so gentle when they met, more, he'd answered every question she'd put to him and more. Better yet, he'd listened attentively when she spoke. He asked her about life on the Morar ship, and how that was working out for her.

She'd lost her companion in the event that brought the Maccay to this part of the galaxy, and she'd been lonely of late. This huge SUVI had shown a genuine interest in her and she'd liked that, a lot. The big super SUVI had a gentle side. His soft spoken attentiveness had eased her anxiety and captured her attention. Now, how was she going to get more time with him? When he contacted her to partner with him in the obstacle course she jumped at it.

A few days later, Suvi 19 leaned against the wall, dragging great heaving breaths into his lungs. A Maccay woman leaned against his arm, also gasping for breath. "You're a madman, Nineteen."

"We did it, Leela."

"You mean you did it."

"No, girl. Without you I'd still be back in there trying to figure out how to get past that wall. Blast that Edran. That has their twisted mind written all over it."

"I heard that," came a giggle from nearby.

"Edran, we should make you go through this," gasped Leela.

"Oops, I have to get back to work now."

Nineteen chuckled at that. "Good job, Edran, all of you. What was our time?"

"Four hours, seventeen minutes," grinned Ebony. "The Admiral and Captain Moore beat you by less than two minutes. I'd say we're ready to go with the test crew of four."

"I'll let them know to rest up tonight," grinned Nineteen. "Come on, Leela, I'll see if I can get us into Simple Pleasures before I take you home."

"Deal, take me away."

Next afternoon four people of four different species sat gasping for air and grinning. "Well, how did we do?" asked Denny.

The woman at the desk smiled as she consulted her figures. "You had the best time so far by three minutes, but you lose two minutes for that wall falling."

"You mean the one that nearly fell on poor old Denny?" grinned Sha'tak.

"Yeah, thanks for pulling me out of the way," chuckled Denny. "I'd still be back there trying to dig myself out."

"Yes, and without Mesera and Menaldo working out those dang puzzle traps we'd still be back there at that giant wall. Denny, this was a great idea."

"This was your idea?" asked Mesera. "Oh, beware human, there will be payback."

They all laughed at that. "I am duly warned. Okay, how about we hit the mess and destroy the desserts, I say we've earned it."

"Can't argue that," grunted Menaldo as he rose to his feet and offered his hand to Mesera. "Besides, it's traditional on my ship. Let's go."

"You're the gunner on Friendship, right?" she asked as she linked her arm through his.

As they led the way Sha'tak grinned. "She'll pick his brain dry before he knows what happened."

"Doesn't look like he minds," chuckled Denny. "I sure hope they've got some of that Earalithian tea cake left."

* * * * *

Admiral Sorenson and Vice-admiral Drake were in Simple pleasures when Ebony arrived with her companion. "Ebony, Brie, please, join us."

"With pleasure, Admiral."

"So tell me, Ebony, what's the good word. Both of you are grinning like you're busting."

"It's about the living library, Admiral," replied Ebony. "Tell her, Brie."

"Well, I took a chance there, but it paid off. I saw one of Orca crew come in and ask for a Morar to talk to. I sent him the guy he fought with in that last brawl on the commons. I recognized them as I was one of those too close to the action when the fight broke out.

"Anyway, those two hard heads hit it off and became good buddies. The guy from Orca came up with the idea for the obstacle course because his Morar friend was missing something like that from his home world. The big bonus is, that course is becoming a special challenge for all the crews."

"Oh? Do tell."

Ebony chuckled. "The two original combatants recruited a Maccay and an Earalith as teammates for the obstacle course. Now teams of four species are competing for best times in there. So far SUVI 9's team has the best time, but I think he loaded the dice a bit."

"Oh?"

"Yeah, he chose Captain Ka'ron and Captain Singh for team mates as well as Tagora from Friendship. The course requires puzzle solving skills as well as speed and strength. Nine's got the strength, both Ka'Ron and Captain Singh are hardened athletes, and Tagora is a whiz at solving puzzles."

Jeannie chuckled at that. "Yeah, plus Nine's specialty is finding hidden things, like the secret passageway through that damned wall. I'll bet that was Edran's idea."

Both Ebony and Brie laughed at that. "It was," grinned Ebony. "The location of the entrance changes every time someone goes through so there's no easy run a second time."

"Okay, so it's working well," said Amanda, "but I get the sense there's more. Ebony is far too pleased with this."

"You're right, I am. It's the friendships developing between the crews, the different species. As a bonus, a number of the folks from the Caverns helped us build it and they're running the thing, maintaining it, keeping the times, stuff like that. They're having fun with it too."

"Ebony, you're amazing," said Jeannie. "I should promote you to my job."

"Sorry, Admiral, I know what you're up to. I've seen that new ship they're building, and I really want a crack at flying her. If I take your job, then you get to go play in the new ship. Uh-uh, I like my job just as it is."

"If you're going to fly that ship then you'll want a crew of SUVI, you know, folks who can take the speeds and turns."

"Oh no you don't, Jeannie Sorenson, you two savages aren't leaving me and Brie with the work while you go running off to play in that new ship," grinned Amanda.

"It was worth a shot," smiled Jeannie, winking at Ebony.

While the admiral and friends were enjoying a few moments and a load of delicious treats, an old man sat in his quarters aboard the Orca. A tired smile creased his lips are he replayed the events of the day. One of the gun crew, a young brash fellow, had tripped over old Sven's broom. In the attempt to help him catch his balance they'd both fallen.

Instead of the berating and abuse Sven expected, the young man helped him to his feet, asked if he was hurt, and apologized for knocking him down. Sven had also apologized, admitting his mind had been elsewhere. When pressed he'd said he was working on a chess problem. The youngster had asked what that was, and eventually asked if Sven would teach him to play.

Over thirty years working in maintenance and for the first time someone had actually thanked him for his service and admitted that without folk like Sven to keep things running smoothly no ship could fly. He wanted to learn chess as well. With a smile of bemusement, Sven began to work out a teaching plan.

Rebuked

As darkness fell the Marienas gathered. The fear and confusion were near panic levels. What had gone wrong? What could have possible gone wrong? "Mourana, help us, tell us what happened, what we must do."

"Calmly, people, we must remain calm. If we panic, they could destroy us all. Yes, what happened. All was going as planned, then new ones arrived, ones like the first, and yet different. They were strong, but unable to communicate. We began the testing, but suddenly realized they were seeking the day gardens.

"With that understanding fear claimed us, and that somehow enabled them to see us for we could no longer maintain the cloak. They hurt us with their weapons, and yet did not use the burning weapons we fear the most.

"Once discovered we knew we could no longer hide the gardens from them, and so we fled leaving the warm sun and sweet soil behind. Into the caverns of the Gorthas we went, and they did not follow us there. Perhaps they were unable to do so, or perhaps they had no desire to. It is my belief they were intent on finding the gardens, nothing more."

"But why?" The question rolled through the collective mind link. "What would that knowledge gain them?"

"I have no idea, but I fear the possibilities."

"Possibilities?"

"If the one who communicates returns with greater demands, she can use the threat of disturbing the gardens to get what she wants."

"But we have moved the gardens."

"Ours, yes, but we cannot move the gardens of the young. If they find those, they will be able to hold a terrible power over us."

"We must not allow that to happen. Mourana, what must we do?"

"As much as possible has been learned from the testing. This much we know, the one who communicates and those like her are the strongest, and therefore the greatest threat. The rest are much weaker and will be easily dealt with. We can no longer afford to continue the testing, we must apply full pressure, drive them away."

"What if we can't? We will not serve them."

"Sadly, my people, we may not have a choice. We must now retreat deeper into the caverns the Gorthas left behind, find the infernal machines they had, and use them against the invaders before they find the gardens of the young."

"And if that doesn't have the desired effect?"

"Then we will submit to service to keep them away from the gardens. The communicator promised us they would leave once they have what they came for."

"What did they come for?"

"Food and supplies from the ruins of what the Gorthas left behind."

"Let them have it. Let us hide from them until they have their fill and depart."

"And what of the young in the hidden gardens, they cannot run and hide. Do we not defend them?"

"Mourana, guide us."

"We will hide ourselves from the invaders unless they threaten the gardens of the young. We will focus on the machines of the Gorthas to use as a last resort."

"It is agreed." With that the Marienas began the migration to a different section of the ruins. Slowly, throughout the night they marched into a huge underground warehouse.

The sun rose and set again, yet the invaders did not return. The Marienas marched through the next night until as many as could be hidden were within the building. The rest withdrew into the forests to hide as best they could. Another day came and went with no further sign of the invaders.

"Mourana, perhaps they have what they came for and have gone."

"We can only hope, but I have a bad feeling about this. They're waiting for something, and I doubt we'll enjoy whatever it is."

"Mourana, we all must soon return to nourish in the light of the sun and soil. We cannot remain here in darkness for much longer."

"I know. I will go forth to see what I can learn of them and their whereabouts when the sun returns."

* * * * *

While the Marienas regrouped, aboard the Orca a small meeting was held. "Hi guys, sorry I'm late." The others waited while SUVI 19 settled into his chair.

"Stop by the Kreenon to see your girlfriend?"

Nineteen grinned. "Got a death wish, Denny?" That brought chuckles all around. "So, it's been a couple of weeks now, how does it feel to live like a SUVI?" Nobody answered for a moment. "Denny?"

With a sigh, he responded. "It's a bit weird, Nineteen, and I have to admit, a bit of a challenge at times, especially when somebody gives you attitude. However, I'll admit I've made a few new friends, especially with the other races. I think I'm getting the hang of it."

Nineteen nodded. "Care to share how you got those bruised knuckles?"

"It was one of our own guys, gave me big attitude. I tried to walk away, but he started getting off course. Told me he planned to go into the obstacle course with an Earalith and leave them in there under a pile of rubble. I tried to explain to him the idea was to work together, protect each other in there, there, and everywhere else."

"So, what happened?"

"He truly wasn't getting it, so I explained the error of his ways SUVI style, you know, like you did for us that day."

Nineteen chuckled. "Did he survive? No, wait, that was Axel, the fighter pilot, right?"

"Yeah, it was. How did you know?"

"The black eyes were a clear giveaway. Now, tell us some of the good stuff. What have you learned from this experiment so far?"

"Well, I learned that most of those folks are just that, people trying to survive and make a life worth living. Sha'tak said it best. His chief said we're going and here he is, he didn't get a vote, none of us did."

"So, you're buddies with a Morar now?"

Denny chuckled at that. "Yeah, I'd have to say I am. Those guys are a lot stronger than they look, that damn wall was caving in, and he hauled me up and over with one hand. And that Maccay woman, the way she figured out those puzzles, oh, and Menaldo the Earalithian gunner, that guy has lightning fast reflexes.

"Yes, Nineteen, this whole exercise has been educational to say the least. I get it, nobody's superior to anyone else, and nobody gets a free ride, we all have to watch each other's backs, all the time."

"I'm proud of you all, but Denny, that obstacle course idea was a big winner. So, anybody else? Gordie, what was that I saw in the hallway outside the mess the other day?"

The man laughed at that. "I was running late that morning on the way to the mess for breakfast. A guy from maintenance was sweeping the floor and I tried to jump over the broom just as he tried to jerk it out of my way. I fell on my ass and so did he as he tried to help me up. Poor guy almost went into shock when I stood him up and apologized to him, asked if I'd hurt him."

Nineteen smiled and nodded. "Why did you do that? He was just another maintenance man getting in the way of a warrior."

"Yeah, yeah, never going to live that one down, am I? Yes I'm on gun crew, but we can make a mess and we always leave it for someone else to clean up, guys like him. He doesn't have the glam job, but without those guys we'd be up to our asses in clutter within a week.

I helped him back up, made sure he was okay, then thanked him for doing a great job. I think I scared him."

"Why did you thank him, Gordie?" asked another.

"It's part of that SUVI lifestyle, right? The man has a thankless job, no glamor, no real respect for him, just clean up the mess and stay out of the way. I wanted to see if I could brighten his day."

Nineteen was grinning at him. "Did it work?"

"Yeah, it did. I saw him dancing with that yard-wide broom as he walked away. This truly is weird, the stuff you've got us doing, but it grows on you. I'm with Denny on this one, we don't have to take attitude, but we do have to respect everybody else. I went through that obstacle course. In there you learn quick that every race has a place, assets to help the team succeed.

"I also saw pretty clearly that we were the guys with the attitude."

Nineteen was smiling. "Guys, I have to say I'm proud of you. Now, tell me how the other men are reacting to the new you?"

Another man chuckled. "They're confused as hell, and slinging that old attitude, but since Denny explained it to one of them, they're being cautious. A few are curious and starting to ask questions. We tell them to try out the library or sign on for a team to go through the obstacle course. A few have tried it out."

"I'm curious, what do you tell them when they ask questions about what you're doing?"

"We tell them we're the elite fighters of the fleet, and our purpose is to defend the fleet and all her people, defend them so they can have good lives, not make them hate us for being arrogant assholes. We tell them the idea is to make life better for the whole fleet, even if we have to do it one person at a time. The people of the fleet aren't the enemy, they're our friends and family, they deserve our respect and help."

"As I said, I'm extremely proud of you men. I warned you this would be a lot harder way to live, but you've all stepped up. Let's keep it going ..."

"All crew to their station, prepare for flight."

"And so to work. Keep up the good work and we'll get together a week from now."

* * * * *

"What's going on?" asked Ten and she and Soren joined several of their friends for a meal.

"Apparently the Marianas are up to something," replied Ettlan. "Recovery 2 was harvesting grain in one of those clearings when some kind of machinery came rolling toward them. Captain Baris called everybody in and they lifted off. The admiral sent Retriever and F1 down for a look to see what's up."

"This is getting out of hand," sighed Ten, "and it'll only get worse. We need to talk to them and ..."

"Whoa there, super woman, you're not going down there again. You're still not fully recovered from the last time you talked to them."

"Harlan should have the new armor ready by now, and ..." Ten stopped speaking and started to grin at the fierce little warrior giving her the frown face stare.

"No."

"Soren."

"No. Ten I don't want them to hurt you again."

"They won't be able to, honey; not if I have the new armor."

Soren sighed and relented. "Why Ten, why do you care? Why are you so intent on saving them?"

"They're a unique species, like the SUVI. Don't they deserve a chance to survive?"

"Do they really?"

"Yes, they do, but my reason for going back is different now."

"Care to share with a friend?" asked Soren.

"They lied to me, honey, manipulated me, and hurt me for no reason. I lived with that kind of thing for seventeen years on Elysium, no more. This time I want to explain to them what will happen to them if they try to interfere with us again, and I want to demonstrate the power of the weapons myself. I'm not a slave any longer, I don't have to accept that kind of treatment from anybody or anything, plant or animal."

"Now that's my sister," grinned Nine. "Let's talk to Five about it. Maybe we can ask for Soren and Tagora to work the sensors on F1 so we can be your ride down and back."

Ten gave him an answering grin then turned her attention back to Soren. "Listen to me now, my fierce protector. I believe they deserve a chance to survive, and I want the chance to demonstrate the only way for them to do that is to pull back and make nice until we're ready to leave. It's the only chance they have at this point. I know Five well enough, if we're making new armor she's done playing around.

"Honey, I know this is me being petty as hell, but I want to be the one to tell them to back off or else."

Soren sighed and nodded. "I can't blame you for that, Ten. I'd want that too if it had been me. Nine, promise me you guys won't let her get hurt again."

"I swear it, Soren. I'll talk to Five myself. We've got those sensor settings of yours and Six will be on the guns at all times. The first hint of anything going wrong and he'll blow them halfway to Elysium."

"I still don't like it, Ten, but I know you want to do this. I won't make a fuss anymore."

"Soren, if you truly feel that strongly, I won't ask to go."

"You really mean that, don't you?" asked Soren, gazing into Ten's eyes.

"Yes, I do."

Soren gazed at her for a moment longer then spoke. "No, my super SUVI, if you want some payback, I have no right to say no. Just promise me you'll be careful."

"I swear it; I'll be super careful."

* * * * *

Darkness fell and the Marienas emerged to gaze at the sky once again. Rumblings of thought ran through them until a clear idea was expressed. "Mourana, they fled from the old machines of the Gorthas. Perhaps we have driven them off."

"I doubt that. I have no idea why they fled from the machine, but I do believe they will return. I'm starting to believe that we made a grave error from the beginning with these strangers."

"Tell us, Mourana, where did we go wrong?"

"We should never have tested the one that communicates. Perhaps we should not have tested them at all."

This brought a great flurry of fear and confusion. "Not test them? If we had not tested them, we would not have known how to defeat them. The testing has proven invaluable so many times in the past. Look now at how few plant eaters remain, and how easily they are controlled, kept away from the gardens of the young. There must be testing."

"No, not in this case. My people, you see what has happened, you know what these beings are capable of."

"It was only a threat, only a vision in that one's mind. We have no proof."

"Did they not find the day gardens? Even with a full mind shield they were able to find the gardens, more, they were able to pierce the shield and see into it, use their weapons through it to harm us?"

"Harm us, yes Mourana. They tested us, but the few tested easily recovered from the testing. Why should we fear them?"

"That was only a warning test, my people. Next time they will bring the fire."

"Are you so certain?"

"Sadly, I am. We should leave this place to the invaders."

"But the young in their gardens, we cannot move them. What of the young?"

"I believe the invaders will move on, then we can establish new groves for the young. With luck they won't find the young, for they seem to have no interest. They only want to harvest the fields of death."

Another great rumbling of thought and confusion followed before they settled down. "Mourana, you have failed us, and we believe the invaders have taken you over, for your thoughts run in their favor. You must now withdraw, Brunoran will guide us now."

"If that is the desire of the many I will comply. Brunoran, I wish you far greater success than I had." With that Mourana moved away, shielding her thoughts from the many. A few chose to follow her, and she led them back toward the place where she had sprouted, far from the lands the aliens seemed to desire.

While Mourana moved away the rest of the Marienas gathered near the field of death the aliens wanted and began searching the memories left to them by the ancestors. They searched for the ways the ancestors had driven the Gorthas from this world.

Armored

An older man sat humming to himself as he worked. His workshop looked like organized disarray, but he knew exactly where everything was. He glanced up and smiled as a shadow crossed his workbench. "Hey, Jake. Haven't seen you in a while."

"Hi, Harlan. Yeah, this job of First Officer is a lot busier than I'd like most days. How's that special armor coming?"

"I've got two sets ready and tested as best I can. However, if those dang plant things are doing something else besides what was in those specs you gave me ..."

"I know, Harlan, I know. You can only work with what intel we've got and hope for the best. I'll let the captain know you have two ready."

"Give me another day and I can have four more ready to go."

"Keep at it, my friend. I'll let the captain know and she can pass it along to the admiral."

"Hey, Jake."

"Yeah?"

"If you ever need a place to hide out for a while, you know you're welcome company."

Jake While chuckled at that. "Put the kettle on for tea, Harlan. I'll be back in a jiffy."

Good to his word Jake returned minutes later just as Harlan was making the tea. "Same as usual, Jake?"

"Same as usual." Harlan mixed the tea and passed it to him.

"So where's mine?" came a rich feminine voice.

"Looks like the wife tracked you down, Jake," chuckled Harlan as he mixed another mug of tea and passed it to SUVI 20.

She thanked him then sat on the edge of his work bench. She lightly fingered the material then nodded. "This the special armor?"

"Yes ma'am, indeed it is."

"Got one to fit me?"

"You know I do."

Jake sighed and looked at his wife. "Twenty, what are you up to?"

"I have a strong sense Ten will want to go back down there even though she's not fully recovered. If she does, I'm going as bodyguard."

"Twenty ..."

"I'll take the strikers with me, lover, don't worry."

"Can't help it. I worry every time you go on the warpath."

"I know, Jake, but those damned things hurt her deliberately. She told them up front that if they didn't want us there then all they had to do was say so. Did they tell us to go away? No, instead they tortured her."

"So why is she so fired up to go back there?" asked Harlan.

"She's the only one who can communicate with them," said Jake, "but I don't think the admiral cares about that anymore."

"No," sighed Twenty, "this time it's all Ten."

"But why? There's nothing about the greater good going on here now."

Twenty shook her head and sighed. "I know, and so does Ten. I don't think our magic gardener has the greater good in mind anymore, as far as the Marienas are concerned. I'm fairly sure this is about payback."

"Can't blame her for that," said Harlan.

"Me either," agreed Jake. "Twenty promise me you'll be careful."

"I will, honey, that's why I came to make sure Harlan makes some of that armor in my size."

"I always do," chuckled Harlan. "So, SUVI 10 who's about six foot tall plus you and the strikers?" Twenty nodded. "Okay, I've got all the specs. Give me two days and I'll have it ready."

"Awesome," grinned Twenty. "I'll drag Jake out of here so you can work." She reached down to take Jake by the arm. "Come on honey, Carla wants you to bake another cake tonight." He groaned elaborately and rolled his eyes as she led him away, followed by Harlan's laughter.

* * * * *

Jeannie sat listening to SUVI 20 and nodding. "Yes, I agree, Twenty. I too have the impression Ten wants to go back and set a few things straight with the Marienas. I guess I can't blame her for that. She went through hell trying to make certain they wouldn't start the hostilities, trying to keep as many of them alive as possible, and they tortured her for it.

"Harlan tells me the armor is almost ready. I told him to make a suit for me, but he said you had already spoken for the bodyguard job. Are you sure about this?"

"I'm sure, Jeannie, but if possible, I'd like to steal a couple of Linsey's crew for this run."

"The two women who figured out the sensors setting to fine the Marienas?"

"Yes, Soren and Tagora."

"You've got it, and I'll send F1 along as well. We're done playing with this. Had they said no at the beginning we would have moved on, but they secretly attacked our envoy of peace, repeatedly. Take whoever you need and do what you have to do and know this. If they drive you back the Orca will raze everything for miles around, except the grain fields we need."

* * * * *

Soren sat on the edge of the bed in her quarters, lost in thought. A soft tapping at the door brought her back to reality. "Come in." The door opened and her best friend entered. "Oh, hi Taggie, what's up?"

Tagora chuckled as she sat beside her friend. "Funny, I just came to ask you the same question."

"Huh?"

"You weren't at the mess earlier, and I saw Ten going somewhere with no Soren attached to her side."

Soren gave a weak smile at that. "She's gone down to the armory to get a fitting with the new armor. By all the spirits, I wish she'd give this up and let someone else go, but she's determined, SUVI determined."

"Yeah, pretty hard to change a SUVI's mind if they get stubborn, but as I recall, she did say she wouldn't go if you were adamant about it."

"Yes, she did say that."

"And that has you messed up, doesn't it?"

"Yeah, it does, and that is weird in and of itself."

Tagora smiled at that. "How so?"

"Come on, Taggie, she's SUVI, doesn't take orders, yet she lets me bully her all the time. Why? Why does she do that?"

"Because she likes you, thinks you're pretty cute?"

"What???"

"Oh come on, Soren, it's easy to see. The tall super SUVI, third strongest of them all, has a crush on you, and you know it. What's got you messed up is how much you like it."

"What??? Don't be ridiculous, I ... we, well ... oh shut up and stop laughing. Okay, you're right I do like it, and I like being with her, she makes me feel safe, protected."

"And?"

"She makes me feel weird."

"Weird? You mean cherished?"

"Yes, that. Taggie, I've always felt valued by you, but this is a lot stronger. No one has ever made me feel like this before."

"And that scares you, right?"

"Yeah, it does. I mean, what do I do now?"

Tagora hugged her shoulders gently. "Enjoy it, sweetie, just sit back and enjoy it. One of the super SUVI has a thing for you and nobody will ever try to hurt you again. Nobody in their right mind would take on a SUVI."

"You're right about that, but what if she stops, finds someone else, or ...?"

"Now you're just playing the what-if game, and there's no way to ever win that one. Talk to Ten, see where her thinking is."

"Oh by all the spirits, I'd be too scared to. What if ..."

"Ah, ah, ah, no what-ifs. If you're falling for the woman, tell her so. I can tell by the way she looks at you that she feels the same."

"Do you really think so?"

"Yes I do, and I'll tell you something else. It looks good on both of you."

At that point a soft tap came at the door. "Soren, are you in there? It's Ten."

Tagora nudged Soren then stood and went to the door. It slid open and Tagora patted Ten's arm. "You two behave, don't do anything I wouldn't do."

"That leaves me way too much room to play," chuckled Soren. "Come in, Ten honey. You get your new armor?"

Ten smiled and hugged Soren's shoulders as she sat beside her. "Yeah, I did."

"You're determined to do this."

"Yes I am. I'll need you to protect me."

Soren gazed at her with wide eyes. "What? How in the name of the spirits am I supposed to protect you? I tried to talk you out of this, but no, my super gardener wants to go be a warrior."

Ten chuckled and squeezed her shoulders again. "No sweetie, I want to go weed the garden. The SUVI have been plotting and the admiral has agreed to have you on the Retriever's sensors. I'm going down with SUVI 20 as bodyguard and the strikers as backup. F1 will be there as well with Tagora on their sensors. Personally, I think Nine has a thing for her."

Soren giggled at that. "Yeah, I think he does. Okay, so for this operation we're using Earalith tech and SUVI superpowers?"

"Yep, and we'll be wearing human designed armor with completely alien weapons. Harlan has adapted and replicated some of the weapons taken from the Wrax ship. Five says this will truly be a Wanderer mission."

"Okay, so I get to go along to watch your back?"

"Yes, sweetie. You're coming to keep me safe. You and I will have direct comms; you see anything you don't like, and I'll blast it halfway across the system."

"Well, all right then, you can go play as long as mamma gets to supervise." That made Ten laugh and Soren smiled to hear it. She so loved to make Ten laugh.

"Come on, little mamma, let's head to the mess for a meal then we need to rest up for the big show." She took Soren's hand and stepped toward the door.

Gearing up for War

While Ten and Soren headed for the crew mess on Reacher, SUVI 19 and his chosen team on the Orca had a visitor. "All right, you guys look like you're plotting something, and I want to know what it is," came a soft feminine voice.

Nineteen chuckled and grinned with delight as he turned to face her. "You always want to know everything, Leela. You're the nosiest woman I've ever known."

The Maccay woman laughed then sat beside him. "Is that so? Then you need to get out more." This brought a round of chuckles at his expense.

"To what do we owe the pleasure of this visit?" asked Nineteen.

"What, a girl can't visit her boyfriend?"

"Leela, if you don't stop teasing me," sighed Nineteen.

"What? What will you do to me?"

"I'll tell your husband then he'll beat me up and it'll be all your fault. Or maybe I'll make you go through the obstacle course with me, see if we can beat our last time."

With feigned fear she leaned back, holding out her hands defensively. "Whoa there, down big fella. No need to get crazy on me."

They all had a good laugh at that then Nineteen tried again. "So why are you really here?"

"Captain Ka'Ron and Captain Singh are working out the logistics for our next group exercise. My husband is sitting in on this one as he is trying to understand the tactics, Ka'Ron invited him along. I came to see my boyfriend."

"You're heartless, Leela," chuckled Nineteen, "and relentless. I think you wanted to get a look at our new long-range sensors and got chased off the bridge. Now you're here hoping I can pull a few strings and get you a second chance at it."

Leela laughed with delight. "As the humans say, busted. That was my evil plan; so, what are my chances?"

"Better than average, by the look on Nineteen's face," grinned Denny as he rose to his feet. "Come on guys, we've got work to do and so does Nineteen."

"Shut up, all of you," growled Nineteen. "Come on, Leela, we won't hang around with these characters. Let's go see if we can sneak you onto the bridge."

They walked away side by side. "So, do I finally get to meet this husband of yours?"

"I don't have one. I lied about that to make sure you behaved yourself. Now I'm telling you the truth because I don't want you to."

"Relentless, utterly relentless," he sighed as he rolled his eyes.

"You like it," she grinned as she linked her arm through his.

"Oddly enough I really do," he replied as he patted the hand on his arm.

They reached the bridge and found the second officer there. "Commander Jones, may I have a word?"

"Nineteen, I see you've brought a guest," grinned Emmet Jones.

"I have. May I ask a favor?"

"The sensors?"

"Yes."

"I see no harm in it, we're not doing much exciting at the moment," replied Emmet. He waved them toward the sensors where the ensign attending the station obligingly stepped aside.

Grinning with delight, Leela stepped to the station, letting her delicate fingers caress the controls as she locked her eyes on the screen. An hour later she leaned back and rubbed her eyes. "Man, that constant flash really gets to you after a while."

"Flashing? What flashing?" asked Dorind, Chief Engineer of Orca as he entered the bridge.

"Here on the screen," replied Leela. "Lower left corner, a constant flashing, slowly getting stronger."

Dorind peered past her shoulder. "I don't see ... wait, I do see it. Dammit to the seven hells, that better not be what I think it is. Please step back and let me work."

As Leela stepped back beside Nineteen, Dorind watched the instrument in his hands and began to swear in Earalith.

"Dorind, what have we got?" asked Commander Jones.

"Trouble, that's what we've got. I suspect this lady's vision is different than ours, so she was able to pick this up earlier."

"What is it?"

"One of the contacts for the resistors we used is failing. We shaved as much as we could to make our rare metals stretch, but it's cost us. We could be without sensors if we can't find more of those metals, especially osmium. I'll contact Moira and see if they found anything useful on the planet."

"Do it quick, Dorind, we can't afford to be without sensors."

"Understood, Commander. Sadly, these are the things we can expect to run into from time to time when we marry alien tech to more alien tech. These sensors have some human, Wrax, original Orca, and a few bits of Earalithian parts."

"What could go wrong?" grinned Emmet.

"Yes, that," sighed Dorind as he reached for his comm to call Moira Duncan aboard the Reacher where all the new salvage was stored.

Nineteen took Leela by the arm. "I think it's time we got out of the way so these folks can work." She nodded and patted the hand on her arm. "Let's head for the mess and find something unhealthy to eat."

She laughed and hugged his arm. "Take me away, big fella."

* * * * *

A meeting of the captains had been called and Admiral Sorenson was pacing, as usual. "Everybody's here, Admiral."

"Huh? Oh, thank you, Vice-admiral Drake. Okay people, there have been a few developments recently. It turns out we can use all of that grain we can get, and moreover, we have a great need of certain rare metals. Some of these we've found in the ruins, but not enough.

"Also, Harlan has managed to produce a number of new suits of armor designed to protect the wearer from the Marienas. SUVI 10 is determined to return to the planet, and since she's the only one of us who can communicate with the Marienas, I've agreed to let her go under the following conditions.

"Captain Sessas, your ship will be her transport and her protector. SUVI 20 will act as her personal bodyguard as will the strikers, all in the new armor. You will also have a specialist aboard. Soren of Earalith, the woman who discovered how to detect them on sensors will accompany you working the sensors. She will have direct open comms to the landing party.

"F1 will ride shotgun for you and will also have a sensor specialist aboard. However, the SUVI won't have the new armor yet, so if they have to leave their ship they will do so with weapons blazing."

"So, it's war then?" said Captain Baris.

"No, Grandfather, at least I hope not. However, we're through playing nice. We'll take what we need and only what we need. As long as they leave us in peace, we will do the same for them. If they come at us again, we'll defend ourselves."

At that point Amanda's info pad buzzed; she glanced at it then passed it to Jeannie. She read the message then sighed. "It just keeps coming at us."

"Admiral?"

"It appears we may have to go to war anyway, Grandfather. Apparently, we're extremely short of a certain rare metal. We've gathered some from the salvage, but not nearly enough. However, it is believed there are deposits to be found on the planet.

"So, Captain Morthel, you will be searching and scanning for rare metals. If you find anything, contact Dorind, he'll oversee the mining operation. Sheila, if you take your people down there to mine, watch them carefully."

"Don't worry, Admiral. We already have the sensor setting Soren developed. Those things won't get anywhere near my workers."

"Excellent. Captain Moore, keep your sensors pointed outward. I don't want anything or anybody sneaking up on us."

"Understood, Admiral," grinned Rhonda as she tapped on her info pad. "It's done."

"Efficient as usual," smiled Jeannie. "All right, Sessas, gather your people and go. If Ten gives us the go ahead then the salvage ships can return to the ruins. If not, then the fighter ships go in. Sheila, stand by, this could go either way."

With that the meeting broke up, comm signals went out and the crews gathered.

Return with Intent

"SUVI 10, your mission. Where land?"

"Back where EX2 first landed, Captain Sessas. Do you have the coordinates?"

"Kumar?"

"We do, Captain. Approaching now."

"Soren, sensors ready?"

"Ready on sensors, Captain Sessas."

"Tentee, got Warmaiden?"

"Armed and ready, Captain," grinned SUVI 20, patting the long-handled hammer that hung on her belt and hefting a new weapon Harlan had developed.

"Ship has landed, Captain."

"Soren?"

"I've got three of them closing fast with more behind."

Ten clamped her helmet in place. "Good. Let's get this done." She swept up her weapon and stepped toward the hatch.

At the captain's nod the man at the hatch threw it open and SUVI 20 leaped out followed swiftly by Ten and then the strikers. Ten marched to the spot where she first made contact and settled to the ground, placing her hands on the soil. "Mourana, are you there?"

"That failure no longer leads us," belled a voice in her mind. "I am Brunoran. We have tested you and you have proven unworthy. Prepare to die."

The being nearest Ten hurled all his malice at her, but to his surprise she struggled back to her feet. "So be it," she snarled as she swept up her weapon and fired. His final thoughts were confusion as to how she could endure so much and still survive, and to wonder at how she could know exactly where he stood. In the next instant the power of her weapon shredded him utterly.

Splinters flew thickly as the Marienas attacked and met their fate. Soren's cold relentless voice continued over the comms. "Ten, two meters hard left. Twenty, five meters a quarter right. Rayla, six meters straight ahead, closing fast. Ten, five meters hard left plus..." So it went until the few remaining Marienas turned and fled. The Wanderers then returned to the ship as the siren sounded the recall.

"Where to now, Captain?"

"Recovery One landing at grain field, assholes headed that way. We go, chase away." The nimble ship rose and moved to the grain site, landing just ahead of the salvage ship. "Soren?"

"They're coming, Captain, about two dozen of them, all bunched up."

"Rayla, on guns?"

"Aye, Captain. Soren, where are they?"

"I've already linked the forward guns to the sensors. You can see them."

"So I can. Ten, marry that woman, she's way too good to lose. All right now, gotcha." At that the guns spewed out laser fire that cut a swath through the charging Marienas. Those who escaped that fate met SUVIs Ten and Twenty with flame throwers. A scant few managed to escape and flee.

"Sessas to Tentee."

"Here, Captain."

"Come back. Soren say assholes run away."

"Understood. Coming home. Come on, sister Ten, let's go home; we've made our point."

Even as they reached the ship and closed the hatch a group of Marienas riding an old farm machine approached Recovery Two which was landing at another grain field. F1 swept in and the machine exploded under laser fire.

The ship landed and armored SUVI spilled out, weapons firing. They didn't have the new armor, but they did have Tagora on sensors.

The speed of their movements and the power of their weapons terrified the Marienas who soon fled. The salvage ships were left to do their work in peace with the warriors watching over them. They returned to Reacher with full holds.

* * * * *

Darkness was falling as the Marienas gathered beneath the trees at the edge of the forest. "Where is Brunoran?"

"Brunoran is no more, his body shattered, his mind silenced by the one who communicates. We three are all that remain of those who accompanied Brunoran. The communicator asked for Mourana, but we attacked. We knew her weaknesses, how to strike, break her down."

"What happened?"

"It didn't work. She withstood the attack and retaliated. Brunoran was shattered in an instant. Horrified we tried to increase the attack but were ineffective. Somehow they could sense us and used those terrible weapons. We used all our strength to hide our presence, but they saw through the illusion. In the madness, we fled but only we three managed to escape."

"It was the same for us as they approached the fields of death. We attacked, but they shook off the attacks and killed most of us. What are we to do now? Who now will lead us?"

"Perhaps Mourana was right to suggest we serve them and survive. So many of us were killed, perhaps this is the end of the Marienas."

"Agreed," came another voice. "It was foolish to confront them. Mourana, help us, what do we do now?"

"Mourana is no longer among us. When Brunoran became leader Mourana left in shame, a few others accompanied them. I can sense them, far from here, gazing at the sky and mourning."

"We must call them to us, ask Mourana what must be done next."

"They will not come. Mourana and companions now fear us as much as they do the invaders. They block our thoughts, our calls."

"What are we to do?"

After much fearful discussion it was agreed they would seek out Mourana and try to reunite their few remaining people under Mourana's guidance. Slowly they set out to find the ones who did not want to be found.

"Can you sense them, Mourana?"

"Yes. Some survive and now seek us to reunite. I am blocking their attempts to find us."

"You don't want to reunite with them?"

"They drove me out in shame for my failure, but now their failure is far greater than my own. They have brought about the final end of the Marienas unless something miraculous happens."

"Mourana?"

"Too many perished this day. We were in decline before the strangers came, and now our only chance to survive may lie in their hands. When first we tested the communicator, it offered us blessings even though we cause it great pain. If we have hope at all it will lie there. We must avoid reuniting with the others until they are willing to understand this."

"Sadly, we will follow your lead, Mourana. You were ever the greatest of us all; we will heed your counsel."

Savoring a Victory

The ships returned to the Reacher, the crews tired and happy. They had won the battle and had no real injuries to show for it. A few headaches that soon vanished with the aid of medication. The captains gathered in the briefing room while the crews gathered in the mess. SUVI 10 and Commander Lilly Peters were asked to join the captain's meeting.

The admiral was pacing as usual and, smiling, the Vice-Admiral called her attention back to the room. "Everybody's here, Admiral."

Jeannie stopped pacing and sat beside Amanda. "All right, folks, let's have it. Sessas, report."

Everyone smiled to hear the Saurian's hissing laughter. "Was success. SUVI 10 go out to talk, Marienas say time to die. SUVI 10 shoot. Soren call out location, Strikers shoot, survivors run away."

Jeannie chuckled at that. "Yes, F1 reports the same thing. Olga?"

"Recovery One and Two returned with full holds, Admiral. No issues and no injuries."

"Excellent. Morthel?"

"We returned to the original grid pattern, Admiral. We found several deposits of the rare minerals and forwarded the coordinates to the Orca."

"Sheila?"

"We have the locations logged, Admiral. Our chief engineer is forming a mining crew which will begin work tomorrow. Dorind's also setting up a smelting operation at the planetary ruins with the assistance of several former colonists."

"Excellent. Ten, what's your assessment of the situation on the planet?"

"I doubt there will be any further interference from the Marienas, Five, but I'd keep Captain Sessas and her crew of savages visible down there anyway. The Marienas now have a lot of respect for that ship."

Again Jeannie chuckled. "Agreed, Ten. Lilly, can you tell us anything more about the Marienas, what they are?"

"With the information Captain da Silva sent me I can give you a few guesses. They were forcefully evolved from an aggressive weed, they are long lived, telepathic, and probably in decline."

"Decline?"

"Yes, Admiral. They avoid the grain fields because they believe it is toxic to them, it isn't, and they've also avoided other of the Gorthas agricultural practices. Certain nutrients they need to thrive were only available from composting certain hybrid plants, but the Marienas rejected everything about the Gorthas and left the cities to fall into ruin.

"Without those nutrients I expect they are slowly devolving back into the original plant from which they were developed. It's just a guess, I'd have to examine one of the bodies and study it to confirm the theory."

Jeannie nodded, lost in thought until Amanda patted her arm. "Yes, well, since we're doing some mining on the planet, we have the time if you want to have a go at it, Lilly. Ten can show you where to find some of the bodies."

The wide grin on Lilly's face made Jeannie smile. "Ten, first thing tomorrow, re-join the crew of EX2 and help Lilly find what she needs. Okay, I guess that's it for now unless there's anything further."

"Just one thing, Admiral."

"Captain da Silva?"

"Can I have the rest of my crew back before they forget which ship is theirs?"

That made Jeannie laugh. "I've heard rumors that some of these characters have been trying to pillage your crew, Linsey. Yes, take your crew back and have another go at those archives."

* * * * *

The crews were enjoying a meal and the camaraderie, chatting happily as they exchanged stories of the day's adventures. Tagora looked up and smiled. "Look, there comes Ten now."

SUVI 9 snuggled closer to Tagora to make room for Ten to sit tight to Soren. "Hey Ten, what's up?"

"I'm re-joining the crew of EX2 tomorrow. Commander Peters wants to study the remains of one of the Marienas, confirm her theory about them. Five said go for it since we'll be here a while gathering rare metals.

"You know, it's funny, I never looked at it before, but the way things have been going lately I'm starting to see something quite amazing."

"Oh, like what?"

"Like you, my amazing Soren."

Soren blushed and slapped at her arm. "Stop it, you fool. Tell us what you meant."

Ten smiled and spoke. "Okay, it's the way the crews work, the people work, everybody doing their job to help the rest, and so the Wandering Fleet continues to survive. We're all different, but we work together to succeed.

"For example, it was a SUVI who first communicated with the Marienas who proved less than friendly. It was an Earalith who discovered how to find them even though they were using mind control and illusion to hide themselves. It was two humans who figured out what they were doing, more humans to find the cure for that and the armor plus the weapons to defeat them.

"Even with that, it was a Maccay woman who discovered the need for the minerals we're mining here. See, everybody, all the different peoples, working together strengthens our chances for survival."

"Can't argue that," chuckled Rayla Mills, leader of the Strikers. "That cold efficient voice of Soren's over the comms today was amazing. Talk about cool under fire. Marry the woman, Ten, don't let her get away."

Ten laughed and hugged Soren's shoulders. "Ah, she won't run away, Rayla, she likes me."

"You sure about that?" asked Soren, leaning away and trying to look stern.

"Yep. I'm SUVI, remember? We know stuff."

Now Soren laughed and snuggled closer. "Well I know stuff too, you sweet nut. Yeah, you got me, I do like you, that's why I went along today, to keep you out of trouble. I was a bit surprised when you went to war though. I hadn't seen that side of you before. Remind me to never make you mad."

"Oh my god, Soren, I'd never ..."

"No honey, I'm teasing. Just teasing."

Ten sighed and kissed the top of her head. "Well stop it, you know I can never tell if you're teasing or not."

"Sure you can, I always confess, don't I? Honey, can you tell me about today. I wasn't kidding; when you went to war, you meant business."

"On Elysium I was the one who tended the gardens on the surface. The SUVI were the only ones with a chance to survive long on their own out there, and since I had a natural affinity for plants, I got the job. It wasn't all planting, hoeing, weeding, and harvesting. There were plenty of animals ready to grab a free meal, and others trying to eat me.

"The SUVI weren't trusted with weapons so we made our own and learned to use them. In a fight for survival you can't play around. I not only had to plant and tend, but I had to defend myself and the gardens as well. I'm tougher than I look."

"She's not kidding there, Soren," said Nine. "There were lots of times I'd be sent out to hunt only to find plenty of meat near the gardens. Ten and I would hang out for a while then carry the meat away where I'd tag it and call it in. An easy hunt for me."

"He always helped me weed the garden before calling in the hunt," smiled Ten. "In spite of everything, we SUVI instinctively knew we needed each other and did everything we could to help our own little herd."

"What was the hardest part for you, Ten?" asked Tagora. "Being outside alone, I mean."

Ten sighed then nodded. "I've never spoken this out loud before, but the hardest part of that for me was not running with the Oraks when they migrated through. That's what made so many infected people go utterly mad. The need to run with that herd was so strong they couldn't overcome it. A few even managed to break free and join that migration, but none of them survived.

"It was incredibly powerful. I always planted on the side hills even though the valley floor had better soil. Up in the hills it was easier to defend the gardens and the migrations went along the lowlands, but the pull to join them, so ungodly strong.

"Remember it, Nine, the two of us standing on the hill watching them pass by and aching to join them, to run with the herd."

"Yeah, it was strong all right," he replied, looking at his plate. "I did run with them once."

"You did? I didn't know that," said Ten, surprised. "How did you manage to escape once you were with them?"

"I got tackled by a hurricane. I have no idea how long I'd been running, two days maybe, could have been more. I was near the edge of the herd when I was tackled by Five. I fought with everything I had, crazy mad to get back up and run, but she held be down. I got loose a couple of times, but she brought me down again, got her arms and legs around me to hold me still. She wouldn't let go until the herd was long gone, then she fed me her rations and helped me back to the caverns."

"Wow, I didn't know."

"We never told anyone, Ten. If First Prime had found out he'd have killed me, or chained me inside the caverns, never to see fresh air again."

"Wow, there's more to the admiral than I imagined," said Rayla.

"From the time she was changed, even though still a child herself, she was always trying to help and protect the rest of us," said Ten. "It's who she is, what she does. You call the SUVI superpowered, and maybe we are in some ways, but Five is superpowered even for a SUVI. That's why First Prime was so hard on her, he knew she was the greatest of us all, and he was jealous of that."

"I can believe that, but look at what she does, how she works."

"What do you mean, Ray?" asked another voice further down the table.

"Like this, Jack. With her abilities the admiral could easily take full control, turn us into some kind of personal slave force, but she does everything she can to keep us alive and make our lives better. For example, when she learned Ebony Graves was secretly helping people find new and better jobs, things they love to do, she promoted her and cut her loose. Same thing with Captain da Silva."

"Yeah, and a few dozen others," agreed the voice. "I guess these SUVI aren't a bad lot after all." There were chuckles all round at that.

The meal ended and they all sought out their quarters for some rest. Soren held Ten's hand as they walked along the passageway. "You're being awfully quiet, sweetie. Is everything okay?" asked Ten.

"Yeah it is," Soren sighed, "no, it isn't. I'm kind of messed up."

"Was it today, honey? Did I scare you when I went on the warpath?"

"No, honey, you didn't. Actually, I was proud of my super SUVI. The damned Marienas learned what happens when you mess with the SUVI."

"Without you they'd have made an end of me, my magical Earalith woman."

Soren sighed again. "And there's the sore spot."

"Here's your quarters. Want me to come in so you can tell me what's on your mind?"

"Yes, but it's what's on your mind that I need to know."

Ten opened the door and ushered Soren into her own quarters. She sat her on the chair then sank to the floor at her feet. She laid her head against Soren's lap and gently hugged her legs. "I'm listening, sweetie."

"By the spirits, I wish I knew how to say this."

"Just say it, sweetheart, it hurts less if you just say it." Ten was preparing herself for the rejection that would destroy her, but she'd rather hear it straight out than try to guess, to be slowly pushed away after the joys of being so close.

"Okay. Ten, I'm scared, scared to death."

Ten turned to gaze up and saw the tears in the woman's eyes. "Oh my darling girl, what is it? Tell me and I'll do anything, anything at all to make it better."

Soren swallowed hard. "Okay. Promise you'll never leave me, ever."

In one smooth graceful motion SUVI 10 rose to her feet scooping the smaller woman into her arms. She sank onto the chair with Soren in her lap, holding her close and laying her head on the girl's shoulder. "I swear it to you, Soren my love, I'll never leave you, not ever. I love you madly and want to be near you for ever and ever. I will hold you to me and cherish you beyond reason until the universe runs down."

Soren clung tightly to Ten's neck, tears flowing down her cheeks. "Promise me. Please Ten, promise me you mean that. I didn't mean to fall in love with you, but I couldn't help it. You make me feel safe, cherished, and I so need that."

"You will have it, my darling girl, that and more, every moment of every day, I promise you. Rayla was right, you're far too good to lose, so here we go. Soren of Earalith, I want you, I love you, please be my life companion from this moment until the end of time."

"Yes, Ten, yes, please let it be."

"Then it is. Soren my love, I know your trust issues, for you've shared that pain with me. Now I'll tell you a secret about the SUVI, but you must keep it secret."

Soren eased back to gaze into Ten's eyes. "Of course. Ten, what is it?"

"Honey, you call us superpowered. Yes, many things about us must look like that. Here's a secret about us we didn't know ourselves until just recently. When a SUVI chooses a mate, she will do it instinctively, and it is overpowering, that need to be near the chosen one. It will happen in an instant and then the SUVI will never be happy unless with that person."

"And you chose me? When did you know?"

"The moment we met. I saw you, so scared and yet so fierce, and I felt the call, the need, like a blow of pure light, of joy."

"Oh by the spirits, I thought you were laughing at me but you were ..."

"Utterly smitten. I went through hell trying to find you. I can't describe my joy at finding you outside my quarters, so determined to hold me still long enough to make amends. Soren, my most cherished, I've been yours from that moment on."

"You know what? I think that SUVI thing works both ways, 'cause my natural instinct would have been to hide where you could never find me. I was driven to seek you out and make it right between us, but I had no idea why." She noticed the sudden look on Ten's face. "What? Ten, what is it?"

"Dear gods, but you Earalith folk are a clever lot. Honey, you've just given me the last piece of the puzzle."

"I don't understand."

"When a SUVI chooses a mate by instinct, for the SUVI that's it, there'll be no other, ever. Our greatest fear is that the chosen one won't want us, or our attentions. Twenty went through hell after they were rescued until they got themselves sorted out. And it has worked out, every time. Each time a SUVI has fallen for a mate, it has been successful, and you just figured out why. In that moment of choosing it works both ways."

"So, you're saying Tagora doesn't stand a chance," giggled Soren.

"Not a hope. Did you see how Nine slid closer to her for a sneak cuddle? They're both sunk and it looks good on them."

"Yes it does. Ten, stay with me tonight?"

"Tonight and every night from now on, my most cherished. I confess, as you might have guessed, I crave the closeness with you, but I have issues about being touched."

"Me too. We'll work it out together?"

"We'll work it out together," smiled Ten.

"Then let's get started." She squirmed around on Ten's lap then raised her lips for a kiss.

* * * * *

The SUVI were gathered in the briefing room of the Reacher for one of their SUVI gatherings. "Ten, are you sure?"

"I'm sure, Five. The rest of you can speak with your partners to confirm, but I believe this is the truth of it. Think about it, you've spoken of what the vice-admiral went through to re-connect with you."

"She's right, Jeannie. Jake's told me lots of times that he was lost without me, and I was sure as hell a mess without him," said Twenty.

"Same here," said Twelve. "Rayla's told me a dozen times, the minute I found her on Igen she was mine, and I sure as hell was hers."

"So it works both ways," mused Suvi-jean. "Looks like you're on pretty safe ground, Nine."

He laughed heartily at that. "Good to know, and a load off my mind. Now, how do I lure her onto the crew of F1."

"Linsey will shoot you, and so will I," grinned Eighteen. "I too can confirm Ten's assessment. Linsey said it was the same for her."

"It seems we're still learning things about ourselves, who and what we are," mused Jeannie. "I fully expected we'd fall for humans who we most closely resemble, but, considering our past experiences with humans, I guess it's no surprise some of us have been drawn to other species. However it goes, I hope it all works out for you, every one of you."

Reconciled

Again, as darkness fell, the few remaining Marienas emerged from hiding to gaze at the sky. Mourana stood with her few loyal companions, mourning the loss of all that was. "Mourana, your thoughts are strange to us, confusing. What troubles you?"

"Forgive my scattered and saddened ramblings, my friends. I simply attempt to find a solution, a means for the Marienas to survive into the next generation. So few seeds now ever reach maturity of thought, and fewer still achieve mobility. With only such a small number of us left to tend them, with none left to teach them, to pass along the memories, the techniques of the testing ... and that was our undoing, the testing.

"Had we not tested the communicator, perhaps we might be facing a different outcome."

"Mourana, can you not hear the cries of those we left behind? They seek us, wish to re-unite with us, to have you lead all Marienas once again. They made a mistake, a fatal one, can you not forgive them?"

Mourana sighed and gazed more intently at three distinct points of light in the night sky, three points of light that didn't belong there. "Is that your wish?"

"There are so few of us left, Mourana. Let us put aside our differences and face our end together as we faced life together before the invaders came."

"As you desire." With that resigned thought Mourana lowered her blocks and allowed the remaining Marienas to locate her. She felt them move toward her instantly. "They're coming. It will be another cycle of light and dark before they arrive."

"Then we will rest in sun and soil until they get here."

Another day passed into night before Mourana's small band saw the first arrival of the refugees. "Sink root, drink water, taste of the soil, and rest. We will wait until all have arrived then we will commune together."

"As you desire, Mourana." The exhausted Marienas gratefully sank roots into the welcoming damp soil. It was another day before all were gathered together. "All are here, Mourana. If any others survive, they are unable to travel or communicate. We are all that remain."

"You have sought me out, here in the garden where I was sprouted and grew to freedom of movement. Tell me of what happened."

"It was horrible beyond belief, beyond understanding. Brunoran led some of us toward the place the communicator favored. Others gathered at the fields of death to attack them there. When the communicator came Brunoran attacked it, but it withstood him. We added our power to his, but it rose from the ground and fought back.

"Brunoran was shattered, splinters of him flying everywhere. Somehow the communicator withstood him and knew where he was. The others with it withstood us as well, and they could see us. They used weapons of terror, slew us by the numbers. We tried to flee the madness, but only a small number of us managed to escape.

"It was the same at the fields of death. They came and used their weapons, killing dozens, yet remained unharmed by our efforts. We had no defense against their weapons, and no way to hide ourselves.

"We fled to the cave of the Gorthas machines. The machines had chased them away before, so we tried that, but they came through the air and destroyed the machine and all who accompanied it.

"The last of us, those of us who have managed to find this place, are all that's left. Mourana, you were ever our most able leader. We made a terrible mistake, forgive us, lead us again. Help us, what must we do?"

"There is little we can do," sighed Mourana. "It was a mistake to test these invaders. We should have listened to the communicator when it warned us not to anger the great leader in the sky. Instead, we tested it harder and the results you have already experienced.

"That one offered a bargain; we should have accepted that and left them in peace."

"You are right and were all along. What do we do now?"

"We wait and eventually we perish. We have brought about the final end of the Marienas."

"Is there nothing at all to be done, Mourana? Is there no hope at all?"

Mourana sighed deeply and gazed at the three points of light once again. "There is perhaps a faint hope, but I fear to try it."

"What is it? Please, tell us what it is, what we must do."

"In the beginning, even though we tested the one who can communicate, it offered us blessings. I sense in that one a great love of plants and believe it may be able to influence their great leader. I will go to the place it favored and hope it will return to speak with me. If it returns, I will beg it for mercy, offer whatever service they may require.

"Do any of you know how fare the gardens of the young?"

"One has been destroyed. The invaders dig in the ground for some reason, and that garden was dug up and tossed aside. The eaters of plants feasted on the uprooted young while the invaders dug through the soil and into the stone below. We have no idea why they did this.

"Go, Mourana. Go to them and offer service, it is our only hope for we can no longer blind their vision. When they begin to hunt us, we have no way to hide from them and no hope of a victory such as the ancestors knew."

"If that is your desire then I go now. Remain here until you hear from me or hear of my death." With that Mourana moved away from the sheltering trees and headed back toward the ruined city in the distance.

* * * * *

SUVI 19 and Leela gathered a meal and headed toward a long table where several SUVI and their companions were chatting happily. "Well, this is a ragged looking lot. What happened?"

"We'll happily tell you as soon as you remember your manners and introduce that delightful young woman clinging to your arm," grinned SUVI 20.

Nineteen chuckled at that. "Of course, forgive me. Leela, this is SUVI 20, the worst tease in the fleet, this one is Ten, there's Nine, Twelve, Rayla Mills, Tagora, and I believe this is Soren. Good people, this delightful lady is Leela, the most inquisitive creature I've ever encountered and the delight of my life."

"A real pleasure to meet you, Leela," smiled Twenty. "Tell me, how did you manage to capture the mighty Nineteen?"

"I pestered him until he surrendered. By the time he figured it out it was too late."

"She lied to me," sighed Nineteen as he sat beside her. "She told me she had a husband, so I thought I was safe."

"You deceived him?" asked Ten, trying to look astonished and failing as her grin spread.

"I did, yes. I asked a SUVI hunter how to trap a large, powerful beast and I was told to set a trap, make the prey think one thing then do another. Poor Nineteen thought I was just being nosey, wanting to know everything about everything, and I do, but I was really finding ways to stay close to him until I could figure out how to hogtie him."

This brought a great round of laughter at Nineteen's expense. He grinned as he put his arm around her shoulders and hugged her gently. "You're a hard and fierce woman, Leela."

"You like me."

"Yes I do, girl, yes I do. Okay, enough of embarrassing me, how did things go on the planet? Some of you look a bit ragged. Ten?"

"Yeah, all right, the new armor wasn't completely effective when they went all out savage on us, but it did the job," said Twenty. "As soon as they started Soren got on the comms and gave us our firing orders. If there was anyone on that planet who was scary it was Soren."

"What does that mean?" asked Soren.

Twenty turned to smile at the small earnest woman. "Girl, you were cold as deep space and hard as steel. That relentless voice kept hammering out coordinates and we kept firing as directed. The Marienas had no chance at all. Their mind fogging tricks might work on a person, but not on a tech wizard.

"You found them, gave their precise locations, directed the fight by giving each of us different targets, and you never once let up or faltered. You were scary as hell, and I'm thrilled you are on our side. It's easy to see how the Earalith built such a large empire. You guys are relentless when you get going."

Soren blushed shyly and moved tighter to Ten's side. "Wow, thanks, I guess."

"She's right, Soren," said Nine. "It was the same for us. Tagora got on the comms and started barking orders and coordinates, directing the battle. We messed them up big time and only had a few headaches to show for it. Gotta tell you, Earalith girls are awesome and deadly."

"So says the completely besotted man," chuckled Rayla. "I can't argue with any of that, though. Twenty's right, Soren. We couldn't see them, but you could, so, in truth, it was you who fought that battle, it was you who defeated them. We were just the weapons you used to do it. They hurt your woman, and you kicked their collective asses for it. Well done."

"There, you see, you guys aren't small and helpless, you're an important part of the whole picture, part of what makes the Wanderers what we are, the ultimate survivors." Ten lightly kissed the blushing Soren's forehead then hugged her shoulders.

* * * * *

Several days passed without incident. Recovery Two sought out and harvested more of the grain fields while the Orca's crew continued the mining operations, her small fighters always in the air, searching with the adjusted sensors for any signs of the Marienas.

While the Orca mined and Recovery harvested, Lilly Peters worked on the pieces of dead Marienas they had gathered from the planet. Eventually she went to the admiral and fleet captains to make her report.

"What's the good word, Lilly?"

"The Marienas are dying, Admiral. Even if they hadn't come at us they couldn't survive a lot longer. I learned from studying them that they lack a certain nutrient, probably a result of selective breeding by the Gorthas, and are slowly reverting to the plant they were derived from.

"Captain da Silva brought me a lot of the Gorthas' research from that time period, and that confirmed what I suspected. What they need to survive and thrive is in the grain we harvested. To survive and thrive long term the Marienas need to harvest and compost that grain, feed the compost to their young."

"We've harvested all we can handle for ourselves, but there are more pockets of it growing wild. They called it the fields of death, but in truth it contains the means of life for them."

"Interesting. You're certain there's no danger to us from this grain?"

"As certain as I can be, Admiral. It is a wealth of nutrients and fiber, and nothing I can find that would hurt us in any way."

"Fair enough. Thank you, Lilly, that's great work."

Commander Lilly Peters left the admiral's office and returned to her own office adjacent to the Hydroponic gardens. A quick glance at her notes then something caught her eye. She tapped out a quick message then went to search out SUVI 10. As expected, she found her in the soil gardens she'd built herself, a place Ten often used as a sanctuary.

"Hi, Ten, you okay?"

"Hey Lilly, no, not really. When that thing came at me it came hard. I fought it off, but it set me back a bit. Dr. Marks says she'll put me in the brig until I recover if I don't stay off that planet."

"The new armor didn't help?"

"Oh, it worked, and without it they'd have won easily, but some of what they did got through. I'm a little shaky but recovering nicely."

"Your sweetheart nursing you back to health?"

"She is indeed, my life is blessed. So, what's new in your world?"

"I just delivered my report to the admiral, and thought I'd share it with you. The Marienas are dying out, reverting to the original plant. The Gorthas bred in a failsafe."

"Failsafe?"

"For the Marienas to remain as they are, they need a certain nutrient found only in the grain we harvested. They can't get too close to it for long, but they need to harvest it and let it compost then draw the nutrient from the composted soil."

"Wow, and I doubt they know that. Interesting. Could we make a fertilizer to help them?"

Lilly gazed at Ten with a raised eyebrow. "We could, but I ask you, why would we? More to the point, why would you?"

Ten sighed and gently ran her fingers along a large green leaf, a sad smile on her face. "Can't help myself, Lilly. Yes, I went to war and weeded that garden, but, you know."

"The SUVI gardener in you can't help herself?"

"Yeah, that."

"Soren will veto that idea."

Ten laughed at that. "Yeah, she will. That girl can be tough all right."

"You like it," grinned Lilly.

"Yeah, I do. She should be getting off shift about now. We're to meet in the mess, join us for a meal?"

"Love to," smiled Lilly. "I'll call Hal, see if he can break loose."

They entered the mess to see Hal and Soren sitting together. Soren waved them over and they joined their partners just as the crew of EX4 arrived. Eventually the chatter got around to the strange happenings on the planet.

"Excuse me, what was that?" asked Ten.

"One of the Marienas," replied the man who'd spoken. "It came in slow, not trying to hide itself or anything."

"What did it do?"

"Nothing really. It came toward us but stopped well away from the ship and the ruins. We were there playing bodyguard for Recovery One. They'd gone back to see if there were any more useful metals to gather. We watched the Mariena, but it didn't do anything. It just stood there, like it was waiting for something."

"Or someone," sighed Ten.

Soren turned to Ten with wide eyes. "Oh no, you're not going back there again. Ten, every time you go down to that planet you get hurt."

"I know, honey, I know. But think about it, last time we went down that one told me Mourana had been replaced as leader then it attacked us. We destroyed most of them that day and the rest ran away. I just wonder if that one might be Mourana, if it wants to surrender or ..."

"Or hurt you again? Test you to see how stubborn you truly can be?"

Ten raised an eyebrow at her in feigned shock, she had that small grin of delight on her face. "Me stubborn?"

Soren blushed then chuckled as she playfully slapped at Ten's arm. "Yeah, well, okay, I guess that was silly coming from me. Ten, I just want you to be safe."

"I know, sweetheart, I know, and it thrills me that you do."

"It drives you crazy though, doesn't it," smiled Leela, "wondering what it wants. It's not hiding in fear, it's approached the enemy that defeated them, and it's painfully obvious it wants something."

"You're not helping," said Soren. "Nineteen, make her behave."

The big man sighed elaborately. "I have tried and failed so many times."

That brought a round of laughter and Leela snuggled closer to him. "You like me, admit it."

"Yes I do, sweetie, yes I do. I guess the real question here is, does the admiral know about this?"

"She knows," came a voice behind him. He turned to see Suvi-jean grinning at him.

"Five, please join us."

The admiral and her lady companion pulled up chairs and joined the group. "Actually, I just learned of the mystery Mariena, and was looking for Ten to get her take on it. What do you think, Ten? Is this likely to be their former leader, and if so, what could it possibly want from us, especially after what happened at our last encounter with them?"

"That's the whole thing, isn't it, Five," grinned Ten. "What could it possibly want? I'll admit, Leela's right, it's driving me crazy."

Soren sighed and shook her head. "You're hopeless, woman, you know that? A sensible SUVI wouldn't go anywhere near where those things could hurt her again."

"She's got a point," said Amanda. "What is it about this that has you so tormented, Ten?"

"Tormented, that's a good word for it, Vice-Admiral. At first I wanted to be fair with them, learn about them, trade with them, that sort of thing. Then I found out what they were doing to me, and I wanted to stay away, but a part of me wanted some payback. I got that.

"I was content then; I'd tried my best and failed to get a peaceful solution as we needed the supplies. We went to war with them and now we get what we need without interference. I was actually happy about getting that payback."

"But?"

"Now Lilly has told me what's going on for them, how they're dying as a species, and how we could help them survive."

"And you want to, don't you?" asked Soren.

"Yes love, I think I do. I am a gardener after all, if I can help a plant grow and thrive, I naturally want to."

"Yeah, I get that. Admiral, if you send her back there, can we go like last time, fully armored with the strikers for back up?"

Jeannie chuckled at that. "Tell you what, I'll leave it all up to you and Ten, Soren. The Marienas learned their lesson here and I'm content to let it be. If you two decide to go back, to help them or not, what we do from there will be your call. If you want to go back, I'll put Sessas and crew at your disposal."

Soren gazed at Ten and sighed. "Might as well inform Captain Sessas we'll be ready first thing in the morning, Admiral. I won't be able to talk her out of it."

"Oh, oh, can I come along too as an observer? I can record everything, you know, for future ... sorry, forgot myself there," said Leela.

"Can't help yourself, can you?" chuckled Nineteen.

"No, I can't, whatever will you do with me?"

"I have no idea at all, but I'll think of something."

"All right, I've heard enough; I have work to do," said Jeannie as she rose to go and offered Amanda her hand. "Let me know how it goes, Ten."

Surrender

The next morning they gathered at the launch bay. "So, SUVI 10, we go back, make more Mariena salad?"

"I have no idea what we'll find today, Captain Sessas, but I'm ready to toss a salad if it comes to that."

They all smiled to hear the captain's hissing laughter. "Tentee go with you, keep you out of trouble. Soren, on sensors."

"Aye, Captain," grinned Soren as she stepped to the station.

"We are cleared to launch, Captain."

"Take us out, Kumar. Ten, where we go?"

"Back to where we started, Captain Sessas."

"Kumar?"

"Got the coordinates right here, Captain. We're going in." A few short moments later the rescue ship settled to the ground. "Ship has landed, Captain."

"Strikers ready?"

"Ready, Captain."

"Tentee ready?"

"Ready, Captain."

"All yours, Ten."

"Thank you, Captain Sessas. Soren, are we clear?"

"One Mariena dead ahead, only one."

"Let's go see what's on their minds, Twenty."

SUVI 20 grinned then opened the hatch. Ten stepped out in full armor followed closely by Twenty and the Strikers. They fanned out to march close behind SUVI 10 as she approached the lone figure awaiting in the open space near the ruins.

Ten approached then sank to the ground, pulled off her gloves and laid her palm on the soil. She closed her eyes and focused. "Are you Mourana?"

"Yes," came the soft response.

"What do you want?"

"I come to beg for mercy and to offer service. We few survivors will do our best to meet your needs."

"We don't want your service, nor did we ever. Why did you attack us?"

"In truth, I counseled against such action, for I feared the result of an attack. It is a sadness for me to be proven right. I was shamed and ousted as leader. My successor did not survive."

"I know, I killed him. It should have been clear to you from the beginning that if you didn't want us here all you had to do was tell us to leave. Instead, you brought great harm to me with your testing. When you hurt me, you aroused the anger in my bonded companion. It was she who directed the destruction of your people. Your people cannot hide yourselves from her eyes, she sees everything, she is watching even now.

"Tell me why you pretended to negotiate with me, yet tested me and brought great harm to me? Why would you do that?"

"It has always been done this way since the time of the great ancestors who broke free of the Gorthas. The Gorthas tested the ancestors and they in turn tested the Gorthas, found their weaknesses, then destroyed them and drove them away. Since that time other species, mostly herbivores, have invaded our lands, but always we test them, find their weaknesses, then drive them out never to return again."

"That was your plan, to drive us away so we would never return?"

"Yes."

"All you had to do was ask."

"I came to realize that, SUVI 10, but I was shamed for suggesting it. The rest you know. SUVI 10, we are dying as a species, few seedlings now reach maturity and freedom of movement. Foolishly we attacked your people and were devastated in the battle.

"We who remain ask only to serve and enough spare time to tend the remaining gardens of the young."

Ten sighed and looked at her bodyguards standing close by, their weapons at the ready. "Soren, are there any more Marienas sneaking up on me?"

"All clear, Ten, just the one in front of you."

"Good. Thanks honey. Mourana, we know your species is failing, and we know why. We also know what you can do to reverse the process. Had you spoken of this in the beginning our admiral would surely have directed us to help you. However, now she has declared you an aggressive and antagonistic species. As long as you avoid us, we will not hunt you."

"You know how to help us?"

"We do."

"Please share this knowledge; we will perform any service you desire."

"I've told you many times before, we don't want your service, and especially now that we know we could never trust you."

"Will you tell me why you ripped up one of the nursery gardens then dug in the soil leaving the young for the herbivores to feast on?"

"If this has happened it was unintentional. For us to continue to explore the worlds of the skies we need certain minerals to sustain the great ships that carry us. This planet is rich in the rarest of those minerals, and it is those we seek beneath the ground. We had no idea we disturbed the nursery garden. It grieves me to learn of this."

Mourana sighed and accepted what Ten told them. "I did counsel the others that we should have continued to bargain with you, to adhere to the agreement you and I first worked out.

"SUVI 10, will you share with me the way to help my people, to help them grow strong again?"

"Why should I, Mourana? After everything you did to me, tell me why I should help you."

"You have no reason at all to help me and plenty of reasons to bring me harm, but I sense a deep compassion and love of plants in you. You have refused my service so I can only beg you for mercy. Please, help us."

Ten rose to her feet with an easy grace. "I'll consult with the admiral and ask her permission to help you, Mourana. I have no idea what she will say or do, or if she will allow me to return. If she does give permission I will return to this place."

So saying she turned and marched back to the waiting Retriever. Mourana watched as the ship rose and shot out into the bright blue sky, slowly sinking roots into the soft soil. "I will wait here and pray for your return SUVI 10." With a sigh Mourana relaxed and sank into a deep sleep.

"All good, Ten?"

"All very strange, Captain Sessas. I was right, that was Mourana, the one I first contacted, the one who almost killed me. They admitted what they'd done, also admitted we demolished them in the battle, then offered to serve us.

"I told them we didn't want their service; we just want them to stay away from us. Then it asked me why we destroyed one of the nursery gardens to dig in the soil. Apparently, they understand they're dying as a species.

"I said we already knew that, and we know how to reverse the process."

"We do?"

"Yes, Captain. Commander Peters figured it out and told me. However, I didn't tell Mourana; I want to talk to the admiral about it first."

"Is good idea. We all here?"

"All personnel aboard and ship is locked down for flight, Captain."

"Thank you, Tentee. Kumar, take us back to Reacher."

"Aye, Captain Sessas." He grinned and pointed at the man at the controls. The ship lifted off and flashed out into space.

* * * * *

"You're not serious?" Captain Sessas and SUVI 10 were in the briefing room with the admiral and the other captains, giving their report.

"Yes, Five," chuckled Ten, "that's what they wanted. It took a while to get it through Mourana's head that we don't want their service, we never did. Their big problem is they work almost entirely off the memories of the ancestors and their battles with the Gorthas. I believe we're the first visitors they've had from outside since the Gorthas left. They came at us, at me, like their ancestors did the Gorthas; they had no other frame of reference."

Suvi-jean sighed and resumed her pacing. "After all that's happened, they ask us for help. Astounding."

"Not so much," chuckled Miriam Holbrooke. "Remember, Admiral, we humans did the same. The SUVI were enslaved, yet after you broke free and defeated us, you relented and helped us to survive."

"So, you're saying there's a precedent here?"

"Looks like it," said Miriam. "They're a dying species, Admiral, broken and defeated."

"And you want to help them."

"It would give our aging colonists a chance to do a bit of farming again, get their hands dirty."

Jeannie stopped pacing and sat beside Amanda. "Sheila, what's the word from Dorind, how long will we be here mining?"

"Another month, maybe two or more before the ore runs out," replied the Captain of the Orca.

"Ten, you say we inadvertently destroyed one of the gardens where the young Marienas were growing, yes?"

"That's right. Mourana asked why we did that then left the young for the herbivores to eat while we dug in the ground."

"All right, this one's your mission, Ten. What do you want to do, help them or no?"

"I still don't like them, Five, nor do I trust them, but they're a unique species, even as we are, and we've seen too many empty worlds. I think we should help them if we can."

Suvi-jean sighed and leaned back in her chair. "All right, Ten, it's your mission, what do you need?"

"I'd like to have a ship to ferry me to and from the planet, plus Commander Peters to advise me. I'll also need a few of Miriam's farmers to help get the work done. Since I'm the only one who can communicate with them, I'll have to do the translating for everybody. Captain Sessas and her Strikers would be a good deterrent against any betrayal."

"Done, Ten. Sessas, your strikers will be the bodyguards for the farmers. Morthel, you will be Ten's transport plus provide her and Lilly with armed protection.

"All right, Ten, it's all yours. Keep me informed of your progress. Meeting adjourned, people."

As the meeting broke up, Sessas, Morthel, and Miriam took SUVI 10 to Miriam's office for an informal meeting. Commander Peters was called to join them. "Are you serious about doing this, Ten?"

"Yes Lilly, we need to do this. In a way they're a lot like us, a small number of a rare species just trying to survive. As I told Five, we've seen far too many empty worlds, and we destroyed most of the sentient life forms on this one. We should help them survive if we can."

Lilly sighed and nodded her agreement. "Yeah, we should. Well, I already know what we need to do, we need to teach them to make compost out of the grain fields then make sure the young get access to that. You said they call the grain fields the fields of death, could be tough convincing them to try it."

"That's my job," said Ten. "Your job is to help Marion line up a few volunteers and get the composting started. Now, I have the toughest job of all, telling Soren what we're doing. She's going to shoot me for suggesting it."

"She's a tough character, all right," chuckled Morthel. "I'll talk to Linsey and see if I can borrow Soren for a sensor tech on this job. She can keep an eye on the Marienas while you talk to them."

"Like I said, they may not be willing to try it," said Lilly. "The first thing to do is talk to them about it. If they're not willing to try it then it's off, we can't help them."

"You're right," agreed Ten. "I'll go down first thing tomorrow and lay it out for them. Right now, I have to go home and face the music." They all chuckled and wished her luck as she strode away.

Ten found Soren just leaving their quarters. "Hey there, you headed for the mess?"

"Yes, it was looking like your meeting would run overtime and Ettlan wants us to be his cheering section."

Ten fell into step with Soren and reached for her hand. "Cheering section?"

"Chess tournament. Apparently, one of the fighter pilots on Orca made friends with one of the maintenance men on the ship. Chess is an old human game, and the maintenance man is good at it. He started teaching some of the others, Dorind loves it and talked some of the other Earalith into it. A number of the Morar got involved, and now there a tournament."

"So, we're the cheering section?"

"Sadly, yes."

"Sadly?"

"In the words of SUVI 9, exciting to play, boring as hell to watch. You can give me a full blow by blow of your meeting while Ettlan goes to war for the glory of the empire."

"Okay, sure, we can do that."

Soren didn't like the sound of that; she stopped walking and faced Ten. "They're sending you back down there, aren't they?"

"No." Soren quirked an eyebrow at her and Ten sighed with resignation. "I volunteered, talked Five into it."

"Ten?"

"Please don't be angry with me."

Soren stepped into her arms and hugged her tightly. "I'm not angry with you, sweet woman, I'm concerned for you, frightened for you. Why? Why do you want to go back there where they can hurt you?"

Ten returned the hug gently and kissed the top of Soren's head. "Come on, girl, you promised to feed me. I'll confess all while we watch the tournament."

They walked into the mess hall hand in hand to see a number of tables with the board games in progress, every species in the fleet was there including the lone Saurian. Captain Sessas had proven quite good at the game. They each gathered a meal then took seats near Ettlan's fan group.

As they ate, Ten related the tale of the meetings, carefully watching for Soren's reaction. She was pleasantly surprised. "I get it, Ten honey, I do. There are eleven of us Earalith, and now twenty of you SUVI. We're all just trying to survive. I don't trust them, though; I don't trust those damned Marienas at all. Promise you'll be careful."

"I promise."

"You'll be there with us to protect her," said Morthel as she sat beside Soren. "You've been assigned to our ship for this mission. You'll be on sensors with direct comms to Connie and Thirteen.

"Soren, I agree with you; I don't trust the Marienas either, nor does our SUVI 10. Ten told the admiral very clearly, she doesn't like the Marienas, and she doesn't trust them, but she believes they should have a chance to survive."

Soren nodded and leaned her head on Ten's shoulder. "Yes they should, but they shouldn't have a chance to hurt Ten again."

"We won't let that happen, Soren," grinned Morthel. "I have no idea at all how this has come to pass, but it appears the Earalith have decided to protect the SUVI, and as everyone knows, once we Earalith set our minds to a task, it gets done. I've borrowed you for sensors and

Menaldo for main guns. Anybody makes a move on Lady Ten they get blown halfway across the galaxy."

A sudden loud collective groan went up and Ettlan's group cheered. The Morar he'd just defeated shook his hand then joined his cheering section. Ettlan now faced a new opponent, Leela of the Maccay. She winked at SUVI 19 then made her first move.

New Hope

The sun was just rising and Mourana stretched toward the light. Opening their eyes, they saw the ship swoop in and land. SUVI 10 had returned. The hatch opened; two armored warriors stepped out followed by a fully armored SUVI 10. She marched to the lone creature standing rooted in place. Sinking to the ground then placing her palms on the cool damp soil, Ten spoke. "I greet you, Mourana."

"I greet you, SUVI 10. Have you brought us hope, or have you come for service?"

"Both. I will explain, Mourana. I have managed to gain permission to share with you the means of your survival as a species. Moreover, I have secured a group of our people to assist you getting started."

"That is more than we dared to hope for. Tell me, SUVI 10, why would you do this for the Marienas after all we did to you?"

"Let me be clear, Mourana, I don't like the Marienas, nor do I trust you, but I believe you deserve a chance to survive and thrive. Let me begin with this, there was knowledge the Gorthas kept from the Marienas, knowledge of one special thing they did when they created your ancestors. This knowledge is the key to why your people struggle, why the young struggle. Without this knowledge your people are reverting to the original plants from which they came."

"What is this knowledge?"

"There is a certain nutrient that you need, a nutrient that can only be found in sufficient supply in one place, the grain fields."

"The fields of death? No. No, this cannot be."

"Mourana, tell me why you call the grain fields the fields of death."

"I must search the memories left to us by the ancestors." With that Mourana went quiet. It was a long while later they spoke again. "SUVI 10?"

"I'm still here, Mourana."

"I have found the information you seek. In the beginning, that grain was growing everywhere. The Gorthas forced the Marienas to tend it, nurture it, and harvest it for them. When we rebelled against them it was in those fields where so many died at first from the weapons of fire. Why did you ask this?"

"That grain was the main source of food for the Gorthas, and it has the key to your survival. Mourana, for your people to survive you need to gather that certain nutrient from the decomposing grain.

"If you wish it we can begin making a large area for composting. We've harvested the grain, but it is the composting stalks that you need. As those stalks decompose they release the nutrients back into the soil where you can access it. According to Lilly's research, planting your seedlings down slope from that grain will help them grow and achieve full stature.

"We can help you get started. If you want we can make a compost area for you, get it working, and teach your people how to do this. What do you say?"

"This is so much more than I dared to hope for. What must I do?"

"First, call out the rest of your people so we can teach them what we do and why. Also, show us where the young are hidden so we can start the process to nourish them." She got no response to that, so she sighed and spoke again.

"Mourana, you don't trust that this isn't just a way to find and kill you all. Please understand, if we wanted to do that, it would have already been done. My companion can find you no matter where you go, or how you try to shield yourselves. There is no place you can hide from her probing gaze. We don't want to harm you; we want to help you. Please let us."

"I believe you, SUVI 10, for you say it was your companion who saw us, showed us to the destroyers with weapons. You did not come here to harm, but to bargain. It was we Marienas who brought the harm, the conflict, and we have paid the price for it. We gratefully accept your offer of help. I will return to the others, share the knowledge with them, then bring them here to work and learn."

"Then I will prepare my people for your return. Journey in peace, Mourana. May your travels be made in safety."

Ten rose easily to her feet and returned to the ship. Mourana was already moving away. "Well?"

"It's a go, Captain Morthel. Mourana will gather the survivors and bring them here to learn the gentle art of composting." Ten smiled as she turned to Soren. "Not a trace of a headache. Mourana was on best behavior."

"Good thing too. My companion is watching? She can find you?"

"Did I lie?"

Soren giggled. "No, you didn't. There's no place to hide from me if I want to find you. After all, I did hunt down a SUVI."

"Yes you did, and you caught her too. So, what are you going to do with her now?"

"Oh, I have an extensive list of possibilities."

"All right," smiled Morthel, "take that back to the sleeping quarters. This may be an explorer ship, but the rest of us don't need to be exploring that right now." Everyone laughed as both Ten and Soren blushed deeply.

* * * * *

Mourana traveled steadily without rest, for this was a journey of hope, not a pilgrimage of defeat. Exhausted, they arrived back at the gardens where the others were gathered. "Mourana, rest now, sink your roots into the warm soil then tell us what happened. You were gone so long we feared the worst."

They all felt the tired sigh as Mourana set her roots then relaxed. "The journey was long, and I will admit, reluctant. I arrived and waited, hoping against hope the communicator would return, and eventually she did.

"She was angry, and justifiably so. We both underestimated her, and the powers of her companion. It was the companion, unseen, hidden within that which carries them to and from the sky, beyond our reach, who saw us and what we did. It was the companion who directed the destruction of the Marienas.

"However, even though still angry with us, the communicator has acquired the knowledge of why we fail as a species, and she knows how to reverse this, to help the seedlings all reach full stature and movement. She has the knowledge of how the Marienas can return to thriving as we once did so long ago.

"The communicator has shared this knowledge with me. Here is what I learned and what must be done ..."

Once Mourana shared what they'd learned there was much animated and fearful discussion. "They just want us to come out in the open, to show them the secret gardens so they can destroy us all, eradicate us completely."

It went on for a while then Mourana called for a stop to it. "Cease this pointless arguing. I once advised you all to stop the testing, to avoid conflict, but you drove me out and attacked them. We few survivors are the result of that action.

"You came to me and begged me to go to them, and so I have; you know what I've learned, what we must do. I now advise you to do as they bid us so we might survive as a species. Hide here in fear if you wish, but when the darkness falls again I will return with any who are willing to accompany me." With that Mourana went silent, their mind closed to one and all.

As the sun set, Mourana rose and set out for the distant ruins and a meeting with fate. The communicator would prove true, and her people would survive, or SUVI 10 will have betrayed her, and all would perish. It didn't matter, they were all as good as dead anyway now. The strangers were their only real hope.

One by one the rest of the survivors began to follow her on the long slow march of destiny.

* * * * *

"Captain Mothel."

"Soren?"

"I've got the Marienas on sensors. Looks like they're coming."

"Better wake up Ten."

"She's awake, sort of," yawned Ten as she stepped out of the sleeping booth. "What's up, company coming?"

"Yup, they're on the way. Doesn't look like there's a lot of them left, Ten."

"You're right," she agreed as she lightly kissed Soren's cheek. "That's for letting me sleep in."

"Even though that one behaved itself, communicating with them still tired you. In truth, I don't believe you're fully recovered yet."

"Yeah, probably not. Still feel like I've gone a few rounds with the damned Oraks."

"This is your mission, Ten. What do you want to do?" asked captain Morthel.

"Might as well go down and get started."

The ship EX2 landed lightly, and SUVI 10 stepped out with her bodyguards to greet the Marienas. At the same time, Lilly Peters was directing the offloading of grain stalks and more. As the pile continued to grow, Retriever landed nearby, spilling out her strike force then the volunteer farmers. School was about to begin.

* * * * *

SUVI 10 strode toward the arriving Marienas then sat and placed her palms on the damp soil. A Mariena approached and sank roots into the ground. "We have come to serve and to learn, SUVI 10. What must we do?"

"You must watch closely what these people do. They will go slowly so you can follow the process. They will begin here, then your people mimic what they do a short distance away. I will remain here to translate any and all instruction."

Ten waved her arm to signal they were ready to begin. Lilly called out instruction that Ten passed to the Marienas through Mourana. "Begin with a layer of decomposing material. Place it on the soil then add a thin layer of the grain stalks, add a layer of loose damp soil, then repeat until a high mound has been built."

The human farmers watched and helped the Marienas construct a compost pile. It took them quite a while but eventually they had it built. When it looked good, Lilly approached carrying a bucket of soil. She scraped a shallow hole beside the Mariena then dumped in the soil and patted it firm. "Tell it to stand on this and test it out, see if it suits their needs."

Ten nodded then spoke in her mind. "Mourana, Lilly has prepared this soil for you to test. This soil is what we are teaching you to create. Our technologies allowed us to speed up the process aboard the ship. Try it now."

Hesitantly, Mourana withdrew their roots from the soil then moved over to the place Lilly had prepared. Carefully Mourana sank shallow roots into the fresh compost. A few moments later Ten heard a sigh of delight. "SUVI 10, this is what you want us to create?"

"It is. This is what you need to grow strong, for the young to grow to the fullness of adulthood, to become as you are and more. Is it to your liking?"

"It is delightful beyond any previous experience. Are you saying that by avoiding the things the Gorthas wanted, we are the authors of our own destruction?"

"Yes, but no longer, for we have shown you the way to reverse the process, to return to what you once were. There is more to learn, but this will do for a beginning. Go now and create more compost heaps beside the secret gardens of the young. The process takes time, but it will happen."

"Thank you, SUVI 10. May we ask what more there is to learn?"

"You must learn to plant and harvest the grain, to expand the fields of life, for that is what they truly are. I will leave you to your work, but our people will help you build the compost piles. Simply go to the place you wish to build it and we will bring the materials to you." With that she rose and returned to the ship.

Three weeks later the Marienas watched as the last of the small ships rose into the air for the last time. As darkness fell and the stars came out, three points of light vanished from the sky. "Mourana, have they truly gone?"

"They have. We will never see them again, as they are wanderers, always seeking new wonders wherever they go. However, they both destroyed us and saved us while they were here. With what they have taught us the Marienas will grow strong again, become many as we once were so long ago."

"Yes, already I feel stronger than ever before."

"Before they left SUVI 10 gave me more information. There is more we can do to help ourselves. We must search the memories of the ancestors, find the ways the Gorthas wanted us to care for and nurture the grain in these fields. We must learn to make them larger, expand them, for as the younglings grow, we will become many once again. More compost will be needed.

"Marienas, I begin to believe the ancestors were wrong. Yes, what the Gorthas did to them was wrong, but what they wanted of us would be for the benefit of all. We must search back, learn the way of things."

A general sigh of agreement passed through the gathered Marienas. "Agreed."

Moving On

Admiral Sorenson strode onto the bridge of the Reacher. "Captain Moore, is the fleet ready?"

"Fleet stands ready to sail, Admiral, awaiting your command."

"Course laid in?"

"Course laid in and transmitted to the fleet, Admiral."

"Comms, fleet wide."

"Fleet wide, aye," replied the comms officer. "Go ahead, Admiral."

"Fleet ahead, three quarter speed." At her command, the fleet vanished from the skies of Mariena, heading for the nearest system to explore the possibilities there.

* * * * *

Soren sighed and snuggled closer to SUVI 10, laying her head on the taller woman's shoulder. "We're interstellar at last. Now you have nothing to do except play in the soil garden and rest, grow strong again before you go exploring."

"What? I'm not strong now?"

"Stop it, you nut. You know what I mean."

"Yes I do, my fierce protector. Soren, my delight, I have no desire to go exploring again, I don't. Yes, I enjoy a walk in the open air, see new plants and helping Lilly, but only after the real explorers say it's safe. I'm in no hurry to go through something like that again."

"Now that's music to my ears." Soren sat back up to gaze into Ten's eyes. "What's on your mind?"

"How do you do that?"

"Stop grinning at me and confess. You know I'll get it out of you anyway."

Ten laughed and hugged her tighter. "I know, but I enjoy the process."

"Now you're just avoiding."

"Okay, I'll talk. It's the way you went to war to protect me, sweetie. The fierce determination, the relentlessness of it both thrilled me and scared me a bit."

"Scared you?"

"I saw that same determination and focus in Tagora too. I think I understand now just what you folks mean when you say it's a good thing we never encountered the Earalith Empire. Superior physical abilities wouldn't be a lot of use against such a clever and determined people in superior ships."

"Ten, I didn't mean to scare you, I just wanted them gone so they couldn't hurt you."

"My fierce protector."

"Hey, you're supposed to be my protector. How about we look out for each other?"

"Works for me, honey. That works for me." Ten smiled again as she hugged Soren tighter.

* * * * *

While Ten and Soren snuggled under the leaves in the soil gardens, the Captains and the admiral met in the briefing room. "Everybody's here, Admiral."

"Thank you, Mandy. All right, friends and family, let's take a look at where we stand with our supplies. Rhonda?"

"Reacher is all topped up, Admiral. We're in better shape than we have been for a while. Looks like we're good for metals too. Moira's quite pleased with the supply Orca's mining efforts managed to produce in so short a time."

"Good to know. Sheila?"

"Orca is all good, Admiral. Dorind has our sensors all fixed up and we're in top shape."

"Excellent. Ka'Ron?"

"Kreenon is well supplied, Admiral. We took some of the time in that system to work on training exercises for the crew. I'm happy to report the ship is becoming more efficient by the day."

"All good news," smiled Jeannie. "Now let's look at some of the other stuff. What did we learn in that system? Did we get any tech to improve our own?"

Captain Moore smiled as she replied. "According to Moira, we didn't get a lot to improve our tech, but we got lots of metals to top up our supplies. The report from stores says we're good for grains, and Alli is working on new ways to incorporate that grain into expanding my waistline. Chef in the crew mess is also excited about giving it a try.

"We've also had some interesting developments aboard Reacher. Ebony's idea for that living library spawned several new friendships and inter species projects. The obstacle course is one of them, the chess tournaments are another. Plus there's been a few unlikely romances, but oddly, they seem to be working."

Jeannie smiled with delight. "People, this is so much better than discussing the latest brawl in the common area. Is there anything pressing, or can we relax a bit and enjoy a few days of R&R?"

"I do have one small issue," said Miriam Holbrooke, President of the Passengers Association.

"Oh? What's up, Miriam?"

"Well, Admiral, we the retired colonists who became refugees then passengers, would prefer a new title."

"And that would be?"

"We think it's time we began calling ourselves citizens."

Jeannie smiled and nodded. "Feeling at home here at last, are you?"

"We are, Admiral. Indeed we are."

"Then I declare it so. All right, fellow citizens, meeting adjourned."

* * * * *

Two weeks later the Wandering Fleet hung in the sky of yet another empty system. The small explorer ship orbited over another barren planet, her tired crew relaxing after a hard day and a meal of rations. "It's still a bit early to call it a day," said the captain, "Thirteen, take a look ahead a few generations and tell us a story."

"A story? From the future?"

"Yeah, Thirteen, tell us a story from the future." His bonded companion, security officer on the ship, bumped his shoulder and winked at the captain.

"You're all crazy, you know that. Fine, I'll take a look ahead and tell you what I see." He sat back and closed his eyes, breathing deeply. When they opened, they were glowing amber.

"I see a woman, she's small, probably Earalith, and she's also SUVI, but I don't know her. She's on a strange planet ..."

SUVI Huntress

The planet's atmosphere was breathable, but its unusual energy field was wreaking havoc with the ship's sensors. They'd lost track of an explorer pod and there'd been no response to the captain's communications. SUVI-Ketha had been dispatched to begin searching for her crewmates while engineering worked on the technical problems.

Suvi-Trey had to be somewhere near, she could feel him, his pain, fear, his resolve to survive and protect his brother, Jorge. Suvi-Ketha stilled her breathing and let her inner vision do the searching for her. She turned her head. "That way, but a fair distance away." She turned and started to run.

The light planetary gravity, added to her SUVI strength, gave her amazing speed. Over grassy patches and tumbled masses of boulders she raced, never tiring, seeing everything as she passed, missing nothing, not even the faint trace of blood scent in the air.

Rounding a huge boulder, she saw the battered remains of the crashed explorer pod. Movement pulled her gaze to the left. A huge creature was dragging the body of a crewman away from wreckage. It looked like Sinjin! She fired her weapon without pausing in her stride. The beast collapsed twitching, stunned.

She realized Sinjin was likely dead as he had been putting up no resistance. SUVIs are usually remarkably hard to kill. "He must have died in the crash." As Ketha carefully lifted the body of her fellow SUVI, she noticed the deep gash just above his hair line. She laid him back inside the crashed pod, her eyes darted toward the blood spattered over the pilot's console. She paused and looked at her comrade's still form.

Reaching out to touch his face, Ketha reminded herself there would be a time to mourn her friend. Using her great strength, she closed the warped hatch. "That'll keep you safe for now, Sinjin, until

158

we can give you a proper send-off." She set a marker beacon for her explorer ship, EX7, to find and resumed her search for Suvi-Trey and Jorge.

The ground became sandy. She found herself on the edge of a great desert; her remaining crewmates shouldn't be that hard to find here. The trail wound down into a small valley of tangled purple grasses, jumbled boulders, and stunted trees. Ketha slowed down, becoming more wary. There were predators about.

The tracks revealed themselves to her glowing amber eyes as she ghosted along, ever wary of possible ambush by hungry animals. The six legged lizard-like thing that had been dragging Sinjin away was big and fast. Another of the beasts fell to her weapon and she moved past its twitching form, settling a fresh battery pack in place as she stepped away.

An unexpected patch of rock was an annoyance as it refused to reveal the tracks of her crewmates, even to her enhanced vision. She knelt and let her delicate fingers explore the stone. The steel shod boots worn by all explorers might leave a mark her questing fingers could find, even on sedimentary rock. There, a smooth spot, then another close to it. A moment to focus her instinctive need for the closeness of another SUVI confirmed the evidence on the stone. Suvi-Trey was that way.

A few minutes later she spotted them. Her friends were a ways off yet, but she could see them clearly, Trey facing off against a large predator. "Why didn't he fire? Damn, the weapon must be drained; he's trying to bluff his way out of this." Ketha poured on a burst of speed.

She was nearly to them, moving swiftly but silently across the hard ground in her soft leather hunting boots. The beast sprang and Trey tensed to meet the charge. The beast's charge missed as the lightning-fast reflexes of Suvi-Trey saved him from harm.

Trey's leap to safety wasn't going to be enough as the creature turned and charged again. As it sprang in to make its kill, he managed to get his forearm across its throat, holding its fangs at bay. The creature snarled in frustration, pushing forward towards his face. Trey was stunned at the animal's strength and speed. "Becoming some creature's dinner wasn't on my agenda today!" He thought of his mate as he struggled to push the creature off.

Suddenly there was the hiss of a stunner then the animal collapsed across him. Trey gave it a mighty push and it fell sideways, twitching on the ground. Not dead, but not in any shape to cause him harm for a while.

With a sigh of relief, he regained his feet and caught Ketha in his arms.

"Trey, you're hurt?"

"Sprained knee can't run. I'll be okay. Did you find Sinjin?"

"I did and set the marker. Here, take my weapon and defend a helpless girl while she calls for help."

Trey chuckled as she reached for her comm. "You're many things my darling Ketha, but helpless isn't one of them."

"Suvi-Ketha to Retriever 7, come in Retriever 7."

"Seven here, you find our lost explorers?"

"Two survivors here with me and one body back at the marker."

"We'll be right there to get you, Ketha. Recovery 10 already has the downed pod and her passenger."

A ship swept down on them, and the hatch flew open. Two medics spilled out and a troop of Strikers for protection. "Mission accomplished, Captain," said Ketha as she helped Trey to limp onto the ship.

"Well done, hunter. You SUVI hunters always amaze me; you found them faster on the ground than we did on sensors. Well done."

* * * * *

Suvi-13 sighed and let his eyes return to their natural brown. "Well, there you have it. Out there, somewhere, sometime in the future, a

SUVI-Earalith hunter will be working rescue missions, the Wanderers still exploring lost and forgotten worlds.

"That girl bore a striking resemblance to Tagora, SUVI 9's companion."

"So, did you really see all that, or did you just make it up?" asked Connie.

"A bit of this, a bit of that," chuckled Thirteen. "I did see the girl hunting, caught her name as she found her companions. Some of us may still be explorers, but our sense of family remains as strong as ever. And I find that future comforting."

"Then that's the one we'll be working towards," chuckled Captain Morthel. "Get some rest people."

Notes From the Scribe

At this point we leave the Wandering fleet to their adventures, knowing they survive and thrive. As well, both the small populations of SUVI and Earalith also survive and expand. For the Earalith it was the wizardry of Dr. Eamon Reilly who used DNA gathered from several different partial bodies found on planet Frigid to create clones of those people.

For the SUVI they multiplied in the more traditional fashion. The virus that created them is still with them, yet dormant. The children born of even a single SUVI parent will inherit the attributes of that parent. After a few generations, a number of interesting mixes of skills and attributes begin emerging.

Perhaps one day we'll take a look ahead and meet some of these folks, see what they're up to as the Wandering Fleet continues to explore a galaxy of forgotten worlds.

And now for a look at a different galaxy and the adventures to be had there:

Novan Witch

by

Prudence MacLeod

Taken

The tall woman darted from boulder to boulder, taking cover behind each in turn. All around her were the pings of projectiles ricocheting off the giant stones, and the hiss of energy weapons' fire. She took a quick glance then faked a leap from her hiding place. Several weapons fired at once.

Had she actually taken that leap it would have been her last. She sped from the other side of the boulder and ran to the next. In this fashion she crossed half a kilometer of battle zone. Suddenly there was a shout and a hail of covering fire was laid down for her.

She raced to the shelter of the overturned land transport ship, and the soldiers hunkered down behind it. "Woman, what the nine hells are you doing here, and where are my reinforcements?" The officer before her was huge, and he was chewing on a tobar root. This told her he had probably not eaten for days.

"I'm Lessa, a healer. I've come to tend the wounded. I know nothing of reinforcements."

The big man sighed deeply and spat out the root. "There are plenty of wounded here for you, just behind that ridge. Use the tunnel, it's safe enough."

She nodded and started away, but he spoke again. "You wear two armbands. Are you both healer and dispatcher, Temple trained?"

"I am." He nodded his head sadly. "Help those you can; dispatch those you cannot."

She paused slightly but did not meet his eyes. "Understood." With that she trotted behind the ragged men and vanished into the tunnel.

The smell hit her first, long before she saw the wounded, or heard their cries of pain. As she emerged from the tunnel they were spread about on the ground, one man working carefully, trying to help them. He himself was wounded, but not badly. Spotting the newcomer, he approached. "Who are you?"

"I'm Lessa, a healer."

"Healer or dispatcher?"

"Both, but I prefer healing. Are you a medic?"

"The medic lies dead, just there, I have been appointed. I do what I can, but..." He pointed to a body in a blue uniform; at least it had been at one time. "He wore a medic's uniform, yet they shot him anyway. What manner of men are these Arlens, or are they even men?"

"They're soldiers and desperate men, as are you all," she replied as she took off her small pack and began to spread out her tools.

He watched in envy as she pushed the nose filters into her nostrils. "Have you more of those, perchance?"

"These are the last," she said as she passed a pair to him, "cherish them."

"Thank you, Healer. Now, how can I be of assistance?"

"The grass is soft here, and there is shade. Bring those who can walk, over here." He nodded and signaled to a man lying nearby. The man groaned as he rose, and clutching his leg to staunch the bleeding, lurched toward her. The man's eyes opened with wonder as she cleaned then sealed his wound.

She sang a high sweet note as she held her hand over the newly closed injury. When she stopped he stood and smiled. Her new assistant looked at her quizzically. "You are more than a mere healer, and you are definitely not Borelian. Your skin is too pale, as is your hair. You're not Arlen either; what are you?"

The recently appointed medic was getting far too curious. "I'm a healer," she replied as she pulled the scarf away from the tattoos on her neck, "of Nara Clan."

Her scarf slipped farther than she'd wanted, for the newly healed man saw what she had intended to keep hidden. "Lady," he breathed reverently as he sank to one knee before her.

"A priestess? Forgiveness, Lady, I beg you." The medic sank to his knees as well.

"Granted. Now be silent, both of you. No one must know."

"Yes, Lady, but to know you are here with us would bring great hope to the men."

"Yes, but it cannot be."

Lessa's attention was suddenly triggered by gunfire, and she spun around. Her newly healed soldier had shot a man lying nearby. "Arlen spy," he growled as he kicked the body aside. A communication device fell from the man's hand. "They know you're here."

Lessa sighed deeply. "That is most unfortunate. Ah well, bring me the next wounded man."

The day wore into darkness as she worked. Many were healed, and a few were set free of their pain. She was moving among the most badly wounded, healing where she could and dispatching those she could not help. Lessa hated this part of the job, but it was better to let them die with a friendly face than alone and in pain.

"Lady, you must leave. The Arlens will come in the night. You must not be here."

"None of us should be here. I have a ship coming soon. Hopefully we can fit everyone on board." Just then the call came. "Ship coming in!"

"Whose?" bawled the officer as he and the rest of his men came pounding out of the tunnel. An explosion collapsed it behind them.

"Mercenaries, Commander. They're calling our colors."

Lessa leaped to her feet. "That's my ship! Call them down before they get shot down."

The communications man got busy, and the ship dropped swiftly to the ground nearby. The doors of the small cargo ship opened and a man began shouting. "Get in, get in here now." The soldiers helped the wounded as they all fled toward the ship.

There wasn't enough room for everybody, so Lessa stepped back and pushed another wounded man forward. "I will remain.

Commander, take as many of your men as you can squeeze on. Send the ship back for me."

In the end, she and the two men who knew her true status were unable to board the small craft. They fled into the ruined city as the ship shot back into the sky and out into space. They settled into an abandoned house and listened to the silence.

The enemy guns had ceased as the ship leaped skyward. Their former position was overrun and, she hoped, the Arlens believed all had escaped. "What now, Lady? Do you believe they'll return for us?"

"We must believe they will return. Our task now is to remain alive and free until they do."

"Yes ma'am, better dead than a captive of the Arlens."

"Better dead than a captive at all." They both gave her a startled look, but she neither looked up nor offered any explanation. For the next three days they played cat and mouse with the search patrols. The enemy wasn't looking for anyone in particular; they were just securing the area.

More than once an Arlen soldier passed them by when he should have seen them. Only a priestess of the temple could have kept them hidden. Slowly it began to sink in to the medic what his friend already knew. Lessa wasn't just a priestess. She was witch trained as well, a high priestess of the temple.

On the fourth day they lost the medic. He had stepped away to relieve himself and was spotted by a patrol. He fled away from Lessa and her companion. Run down and captured, he was tortured until he admitted there were two others still on the small planet, a soldier, and a witch priestess. The hunt for them was on.

For three more days they fled the patrols, evading them. It soon became apparent to the soldier that she was continually circling the area where the ship had landed to take off his companions. She was still expecting it to return. And it did. On the fourth day a squawk came on her tiny communicator. "Incoming now. Be ready or be left behind!"

The ship dropped out of the sky and landed lightly, but a sudden barrage of heavy gunfire reduced it to scrap in seconds. She screamed a protest and lurched forward, and then the lights went out.

Lessa awakened in the back of a land vehicle, bouncing along. She was bound hand and foot with a blindfold over her eyes. A soft groan escaped her lips as she tested the strength of her bonds.

"Lie still, witch," growled a deep male voice, "Or you will be shot. Here are the rules, keep your head down, and keep your mouth shut. Never look at me. The bounty for you will be paid dead or alive, and I care not which."

"Understood."

Lessa said nothing more and just listened to the men. She recognized the voice of her companion, the first soldier she had healed. They were discussing how they would spend the reward for her capture. Fools! They had put unfriendly hands on a temple priestess. Their deaths would be slow and painful at the hands of the Viceroy's torturers. The temple wanted her back, as did the Viceroy, that was certain, but they wanted her alive and unharmed.

Darkness fell and the machine stopped. A call was made, and a small cargo ship began to descend. As the ship touched down, the deep voiced man shot the soldier who'd betrayed her. "Now the bounty is all mine," he said with a cruel laugh.

Lessa said nothing, and in truth, she had little sympathy for the dead soldier. The ship settled to the ground and the cargo door swung open. A man was waving his arm, urging them to hurry. Lessa was herded along and none too gently.

She held her tongue, for she had seen into the belly of the ship. It was filled with children of all ages and a small dark skinned woman. Lessa had seen dark skinned folk all her life, but never one so black. The girl's skin was like fine dark chocolate, rich and silky, her features fine, almost elfin, and her hair black as a raven's wing.

A hard shove between her shoulders broke Lessa's line of thought. "Keep your head down or lose it, you hear?"

"Understood," she stated softly as she lowered her head. At this point he spotted the crowd in the cargo hold and became angry. "Mortan, what the nine hells of Porapix is going on here? Get these damnable children off this ship right now."

That order was not well received. "Shut your ugly face, Mekkan. This is my ship, and I give the orders here. That woman has paid for passage to Elliston, and she shall have it. Come along with your prize, or wait for another ship, as you choose. We're leaving now."

He turned and stalked back into the belly of the ship. "Hekka, get those cargo doors closed and sealed. Jonal, get her back into space before those Arlen soldiers discover we're here and shoot us down."

The men leaped to obey, and the bounty hunter pushed Lessa into the ship, knocking her to the floor, as he leaped in behind her. He barely made it inside before the door closed.

Don't miss out!

Visit the website below and you can sign up to receive emails whenever Prudence MacLeod publishes a new book. There's no charge and no obligation.

https://books2read.com/r/B-A-ZKBBB-VCHRC

BOOKS 2 READ

Connecting independent readers to independent writers.

Also by Prudence MacLeod

Forgotten Worlds
Suvi
Echo of the Past
Survivors
Ship
Fleet
Unite
IGEN
T.E.N.

Watch for more at https://www.prudencemacleod.com/.

Telling a story is like knitting a sweater. Start with a ball of possibilities, pull out one small thread and begin. With luck and patience you will create something quite wonderful.

About the Author

On a far off windswept island Jennifer Crandall sits with her dogs and cats creating fantastic stories for all to enjoy. She publishes as JL Crandall, Prudence MacLeod, and Jenni Leigh.

Read more at https://www.prudencemacleod.com/.

www.ingramcontent.com/pod-product-compliance
Lightning Source LLC
Chambersburg PA
CBHW022117170626
46808CB00002B/756